Dear Reader,

Returning to one of my early books is like a reunion with dear friends I haven't seen for a very long time. In a way, these stories are like a diary of my own life. When I hold one in my hand, I remember where I was when I wrote it, what was going on in my life, how much fun it was to live my characters' love story right along with them. *Renegade Lover* brought me back to a wonderful vacation my husband and I had in Key West—I could almost feel that sultry sunshine and taste the margaritas! I decided to give that vacation to my heroine Megan McLean, except I added a little twist: she is nineteen years old and looking for a weekend of fun. What she finds, instead, is a sexy Australian named Jake Lockwood who is destined to be the love of her life.

The course of true love, however, never runs smooth, not even in our beloved books. When Jake and Megan find each other again six years later, there is only one thing that can keep them apart—their daughter, Jenny.

## BARBARA BRETTON

is the *USA Today* bestselling, award-winning author of more than forty books. She currently has over ten million copies in print around the world. Her works have been translated into twelve languages in over twenty countries.

Her awards include both Reviewer's Choice and Career Achievement Awards from *Romantic Times Magazine*; Gold and Silver certificates from *Affaire de Coeur*; the RWA Region One Golden Leaf; and several sales awards from Bookrak. Barbara was also included in a recent edition of *Contemporary Authors*.

Barbara loves to spend as much time as possible in Maine with her husband, walking the rocky beaches and dreaming up plots for upcoming books. She loves to hear from readers, who can reach her at P.O. Box 515, Flagtown, NJ 08821.

---

### Books by Barbara Bretton

#### Harlequin American Romance

*Love Changes* #3
*The Sweetest of Debts* #49
*No Safe Place* #91
*The Edge of Forever* #138
*Promises in the Night* #161
*Shooting Star* #175
*\*Playing for Time* #193
*Second Harmony* #211
*Nobody's Baby* #230
*\*Honeymoon Hotel* #251
*\*A Fine Madness* #274
*Mother Knows Best* #305
*Mrs. Scrooge* #322
*\*All We Know of Heaven* #355
*Sentimental Journey* #365
*Stranger in Paradise* #369
*Bundle of Joy* #393
*Daddy's Girl* #441
*Renegade Lover* #493
*\*The Bride Came C.O.D.* #505
*The Invisible Groom* #554
*Operation: Husband* #581

#### Harlequin Intrigue

*Starfire* #18

#### Harlequin Big Summer Read

*Somewhere in Time*

#### MIRA

*Tomorrow & Always*
*Destiny's Child*
*Guilty Pleasures*

\* PAX miniseries

# Barbara Bretton
## Renegade Lover

HARLEQUIN®

TORONTO • NEW YORK • LONDON
AMSTERDAM • PARIS • SYDNEY • HAMBURG
STOCKHOLM • ATHENS • TOKYO • MILAN • MADRID
PRAGUE • WARSAW • BUDAPEST • AUCKLAND

HARLEQUIN BOOKS
225 Duncan Mill Road, Don Mills,
Ontario, Canada M3B 3K9

ISBN 0-373-82257-X

RENEGADE LOVER

Copyright © 1993 by Barbara Bretton

Visit us at www.eHarlequin.com

**Printed in U.S.A.**

# *Prologue*

The need to see her again had grown stronger with the passage of time.

He hadn't expected that.

When their marriage broke up and she'd left him for the pleasures her father's money could provide, he had trusted that time, healer of all wounds, would dull her memory until it was just an ache, and not a searing pain.

Instead she remained along the edges of his consciousness, like the ghost of a painting that shadowed the wall long after the canvas had been put away in some forgotten attic. The pain was gone but the sense of unfinished business remained.

"Six years," he said, staring at the brochure that rested on his desk. Six years that had seen him climb to the top, his rise fueled as much by anger as ambition.

By the primal need to prove himself to the one woman he'd ever loved.

And now he would finally have that chance.

She was here. On board the yacht. The last piece of

the puzzle was about to snap into place and when it did he would finally be free of the past.

Everything about them had been wrong from the start. She'd been too young. He'd been too hungry. He had dreams she couldn't understand; she had expectations he couldn't meet. He'd moved too fast, wanted too much, been unwilling to settle for anything less than all he could get. He'd married her the way another man might claim a prize, as if taking her as his wife would somehow grant him his place in the world.

Later on he realized she'd been looking for a hero. Someone bigger and bolder than her father, someone who could wrap her in luxury and keep her safely away from real life where people worked hard for their pleasures. But there were no heroes. Not in this world. And if there were, he sure as hell wasn't one of them.

When she walked out on him she'd been a spoiled little girl, her daddy's pampered darling, a child in every way but one. The passion between them had been hot and demanding, as powerful as a force of nature and even more destructive. He'd never believed in love or the concept of happily ever after. He'd never known how it felt to be part of a real family. Yet from the first moment he'd looked into her eyes, he knew he had to own her, body and soul.

Six long years since their divorce and nothing had changed. She was frozen in time, untouched by life or sorrow, still the same girl he'd loved unwisely and too well.

Yet the face that looked up at him from the glossy brochure was a woman's face. Hauntingly beautiful. Eminently desirable. Shadowed by experiences that were hers alone.

The face of the stranger who once was his wife.

There'd been many women since she left him. Accomplished women with ambition to match his. Beautiful women who could stop a man dead in his tracks. But not one of those women had come close to touching his heart the way she had. He would know her in the dark, her scent, the satiny feel of her breasts, the sounds she made in the back of her throat when he—

"Tomorrow," he said, turning the brochure facedown.

Tomorrow he would see her again and whatever magic it was that she held for him would be dispelled once and for all.

# Chapter One

*Miami*

Someone was watching her.

Megan McLean glanced over her shoulder at the laughing crowd milling about on deck. Women in jaunty nautical outfits, men in blazers complete with gold crests on the breast pockets—everyone seemed engrossed in conversation. Not a single pair of eyes was turned toward her.

The odd feeling receded but didn't quite disappear. She turned toward the woman standing next to her at the railing.

"Sorry," she said. "You were saying?"

"You look green," said Sandy, a travel agent from Orlando. "Do you need Dramamine?"

Megan shook her head. Seasickness was the least of her problems. From the first moment she saw the *Sea Goddess,* resplendent in the Florida sunshine, she'd been awash in bittersweet memories. How many times had she stood on the deck of a yacht, equally as majestic, and considered the event as commonplace as brushing her teeth? Another lifetime, she thought. Another world.

"It's the strangest thing." Megan cast a second glance over her shoulder as she brushed away the hand of memory. "Ever since we boarded, I've had the feeling someone is watching me."

"Of course someone's watching you," Sandy said with a laugh. She gestured subtly toward a woman in a white jumpsuit who stood, talking seriously, with a man in his dotage. "Celia Briscoe."

"From Celia's Cuisine?"

"One and the same. The competition is everywhere, Megan. You won't be able to peel a potato without having an audience."

"Maybe that's it," she replied after a moment, although she didn't entirely believe her own words. Professional scrutiny was three parts competition and one part curiosity, more cerebral than visceral. This, however, was something else. Something more personal, more sexual, a sensation that made her acutely aware of the way the sultry breezes caressed her cheek and conjured up fantasies of remote tropical islands made for romance.

"I don't envy you having to cater meals for this crowd," Sandy went on, adjusting her straw hat to a more rakish angle. "The competition is pretty intense, although I can't figure out why the owners of the *Sea Goddess* don't just hire themselves some fancy French chef and be done with it."

"They have," answered Megan, "but you can't expect a demigod to work a sixteen-hour shift. The *artistes* only handle the dinner crowd." Management—whoever they might be—intended to hire an independent firm to prepare breakfast, lunch and high tea with both flair and attention to detail, American style. This knack for avoiding the obvious had the owners of the Tropicale Cruises sitting on the biggest potential gold mine since the heyday of the *Queen Mary*.

Sandy gestured toward a silver-haired man near the door to Promenade Deck. "Do you think he's one of the owners?"

"Could be. He certainly looks like he could afford it."

Word had it that a group of enterprising businessmen had bought the *Sea Goddess,* a two-hundred-and-eighty-two-foot yacht, from a once-powerful tycoon who was down on his luck. The businessmen had transformed the private yacht into a commercial enterprise. No one knew exactly who the businessmen were, but their reputation for brilliant marketing was fast becoming the stuff of legend.

The *Sea Goddess* was positioned to provide the ultimate in affordable luxury for travelers who wanted the best but didn't want to go to the Riviera to find it. "Yankee Grandeur," the Miami newspapers had called it and it seemed to Megan they were right on target with that assessment.

"Over there," Sandy indicated, nudging Megan again. "The man in the dark blue polo shirt. Isn't that a Rolex watch he's wearing?"

"A knockoff," Megan declared. "A good one, but not the real thing."

Sandy eyed her with curiosity. "You sound pretty sure of yourself."

"I am." Once upon a time this had been Megan's world. Gold watches, diamond tennis bracelets, dinner at the club—they had all been as commonplace to her as

Timex watches, costume jewelry, and lunch beneath the Golden Arches.

This time, however, there was a difference.

This time she was there to work.

The Movable Feast, the catering firm Megan and her partner Ingrid owned, had been summoned on this shake-down cruise, singled out of a hundred other catering firms in the area. Firms, Megan suspected, who were equally as good as theirs. Not that she was asking any questions. She wanted this contract badly, and all she had to do was dazzle the powers-that-be on Sunday with her skills, then pray the other companies in the running bowed to the inevitable.

Megan's freewheeling imagination coupled with her partner's keen business sense had made them a duo to be reckoned with. Five years ago she'd shown up on In-grid's doorstep, with Jenny in her arms and hope in her heart, to apply for the job of Stace's nanny. Who would have imagined that she would end up with not only a best friend but a business partner?

They had earned this opportunity through talent and hard work and Megan knew in her bones that securing a place on the staff of the *Sea Goddess* would move them into the big time. Ingrid said they were doing fine without the Tropicale franchise, but Megan was determined to see it through to even greater success. The fact that they'd asked specifically for her made it even more important.

Strange how much she'd taken for granted when she was growing up. Ballet lessons. Horseback riding. Wednesday afternoon lunches at the club where she'd learned the difference between eating and dining. Her closet had bulged with lacy party dresses and cashmere

sweaters and tennis shoes coordinated to match her play-
suits. Once upon a time she'd believed that was the way
life was for everybody—the way life always would be
for her.

Well, she'd learned otherwise and, to her amazement,
she'd survived. The very things she'd longed for during
her brief marriage, things her husband couldn't provide,
had proved to be unimportant. She could do without all
the luxuries she'd once taken for granted. If only she'd
learned that before her marriage broke up, she and Jake
might have had a chance.

Not that it mattered. The only thing that mattered now
was nailing the contract with Tropicale and taking another step toward securing the future for her daughter.

JAKE WATCHED HER from the uppermost deck.

Six years since he had held her in his arms.

Six years since he'd tasted her lips.

Six years since he'd known the sweet secrets of her
body.

All the places he'd seen, the things he'd done, the
women he'd known—vanished, all of them, in the blink
of an eye. Every cell and fiber of his body ached for her.
Her power over him was stronger and even more demanding than his need to show her that he had succeeded.

She leaned against the railing, her fiery auburn hair a
sleek line against her cheek as she gazed out at the sun-
splashed wake that trailed behind the ship. It was all he
could do to keep from pulling her into his arms and having her right there on the deck.

He wanted to hate her. Everything about her screamed
privilege, from her glossy hair to the expensive shoes on

her feet. She stood there, head held high, as if she owned the *Sea Goddess* and everyone on it. Every casual movement was imbued with an arrogant grace, an elegant disdain that told a man he could look but he couldn't touch.

This wasn't about reunions, he warned himself. This was about putting the past to rest once and for all and getting on with his life.

He'd come so far since she'd seen him last. No longer struggling to find success, he had accomplished more than even he had dared to dream. He had the respect and admiration of his colleagues. He owned homes in three countries and more cars than he knew what to do with. Everything he touched turned to gold and he was lucky enough to have the time and the inclination to enjoy every bit of it.

The sailboat of his dreams, built by the best in the business, waited at the marina in Maui. He could do it now, sail off into the endless sunset while his fortune grew bigger and his future more secure. It's what he'd wanted to do since he was old enough to dream. And now there was nothing to stop him.

Except Megan. Spoiled, selfish, impossibly beautiful Megan. The woman he'd loved and hated and never been able to forget.

And, damn it, the woman he still wanted more than any woman he'd ever known.

DINNER WAS SUPERB, as Megan had known it would be. Medallions of veal so tender they melted in her mouth. The use of coriander in the sauce had been subtle and effective, and she made a mental note to try adapting that technique to her own repertoire. Someone had wisely seen to it that the caterers vying for position on the *Sea Goddess* were seated at separate tables and so she'd found herself actually enjoying herself. Sandy and her sister, Val, partners in a travel agency, had a comically adversarial relationship that kept Megan amused from appetizers through dessert.

"...so if it hadn't been for Val, I would never have taken time to go on vacation." Sandy's husky laugh rang out as they strolled into the lounge for after-dinner drinks.

"She's married to her work," Val said ruefully.

Sandy shot her sister a glance sharp as a razor's edge. "Beats being married to my ex."

Megan said nothing, just smiled absently at the women's good-natured banter. She was glad for their company. The last thing she'd expected was to feel uncomfortable amid the splendor of the *Sea Goddess* but there it was. She'd thought it would be easy to fall into the old ways, downing Taittinger's as if it were water, eating caviar and laughing the carefree laugh of a woman who'd never known anything but the best. But the old ways no longer fit and she doubted they ever would again.

After dinner they strolled the deck for a while then stopped in the lounge for a drink.

"Over there." Megan pointed to a trio of swivel chairs against the starboard wall of windows.

"God," Val breathed. "That view...."

The beauty of the moon's crystallized reflection on the calm black sea was so achingly romantic that Megan quickly turned away. Some things were meant to be shared.

Small candles burned at each table, providing a soft and sensual glow. The dark richness of the brandy, the lush music from the quartet in the far corner of the room—it all conspired to remind her of another time and place when life had seemed so simple.

Even now, on a yacht headed toward the open sea, light-years away from the life she and Jake had once shared, she found her thoughts drawn back to a time that no longer existed. Lazy Sundays in bed and nights of ecstasy beyond a woman's wildest dreams. But there was more than that, much more. There were days when she wondered if maybe, just maybe, they could have made their marriage work. He didn't want to hear about white picket fences and a bouquet of beautiful babies. His background hadn't taught him how to dream those particular dreams.

"A beautiful boat, Meggie," he'd said to her so many times. "With only the two of us for company...."

"Or three of us," she'd amended, thinking of a baby with his golden eyes.

No babies. No children to tie them down to real life. He wasn't father material and never would be.

She smoothed her hair off her forehead with an impatient gesture. For all she knew Jake was back in Australia or exploring Timbuktu, chasing crocodiles or beautiful blondes—whatever his current pleasure might be. Certainly the last place he'd be was on a cushy cruise with a bunch of overfed, overeager businessmen.

No, that had never been Jake's style.

He'd been her poet, her dark knight in shining armor, the renegade lover of her girlish dreams. "One day we'll sail around the world," he'd promised her. Just the two of them, naked beneath a blanket of stars. His dreams had been as wild and unbridled as his lovemaking, and every bit as seductive.

With all her heart and soul she'd wanted to believe he could make the facts of their daily life vanish. But she'd been too young, too spoiled, so accustomed to being indulged that she simply didn't know how to believe in him.

*SHE WAS NINETEEN when they met, Darrin McLean's headstrong daughter. Born and raised in the rarefied atmosphere of Palm Beach, rubbing shoulders with the Whitneys and Posts, she had never seen the other side of life.*

*The wild side.*

*She'd wanted to kick free of the traces of privilege and a long weekend seemed the answer to her prayers. Innocent, petulant, thoroughly spoiled, she'd been more girl than woman, shielded from reality by the cushion of her father's wealth.*

*Key West was everything she'd hoped it would be: slightly tacky, somewhat decadent, filled with possibilities.*

*Volleyball, however, wasn't one of the possibilities she was interested in pursuing. Instead she'd stretched out on a yellow beach towel, eyes closed, listening to the sounds of the ocean slapping against the shore and the excited laughter of her friends as they played volleyball down the beach.*

*She'd been drifting into a light doze when he approached.*

*"Are you asleep?" His voice was rough honey*

*pouring over her. The accent was both foreign and familiar, that blend of British inflection and American energy that was pure Australian.*

Her eyes fluttered open. "Not anymore."

"Good. Sleeping's a waste of time."

She propped herself up on her elbow and took a good look at the man who stood in front of her. Nothing about him was familiar or comforting. He had danger written all over him, from his broad shoulders to the rippling muscles of his chest and belly. Certainly she'd never seen his type on the airbrushed beaches of Palm Springs. Backlit by the fierce sun, he glowed with an aura of raw strength and sexuality.

Ah yes. This was danger. A walk on the wild side of love. A delicious ripple of excitement began in the pit of her stomach.

Smiling with the confidence peculiar to a girl who had never known rejection, she tossed her hair back from her face. This was a game she knew and understood. The parry and thrust of flirtation. The delicate art of promises no one expected you to keep.

He dropped to his knees next to her and she caught the sun-warmed scent of his skin. His eyes were an odd shade of deep amber, framed by spiky dark lashes that made the color all the more striking. A slow heat radiated out from her core.

"Do my back, would you?" he asked. His wicked grin said something else entirely.

"I'll do your back," she said lightly, "if you promise to do mine."

"Anything you want." His dark gaze lingered on

*her breasts, which strained against the two triangles of fabric covering them. "Just ask me and it's yours."*

*No, she'd never seen a man like him before, not anywhere. Everything about him, from his chestnut hair streaked from the sun to his bronzed frame, screamed danger. He wore cutoffs and a wicked grin and she knew that if she lived to be a thousand years old she would never find a man more perfect for her.*

*Nothing else mattered. Not reason or propriety or the fact that they hadn't a chance in the world to make it work.*

*One month later they were married.*

*One year later they were divorced. Clean, neat and painless.*

*Except for the fact that Megan was pregnant with his child.*

VAL'S VOICE BROUGHT Megan back to the present.

"Look at that," Val declared as Sandy accepted an invitation to dance from a balding man with a wide smile. "I would've figured he was on his way to ask you to dance. I saw the way he was checking out that strapless gown of yours."

"We had a run-in on the stairs earlier," Megan replied with a rueful smile. "I'm afraid he can't control those hands of his. The sea air must do something to men's hormones."

As if on cue, a young man in an Armani jacket sidled up to her and held out his hand.

*Be nice,* she warned herself. *His daddy might own the company.*

"Yes?" she asked, as politely and sweetly as she could manage.

"Dance," he said, obviously a man of few syllables. "How 'bout it?"

She upped the wattage on her smile. "Sorry," she answered lightly.

He hesitated, debating the wisdom of pursuing the issue, but she swiveled her chair around once again, cutting short the encounter.

Val looked at her with open curiosity. "A bit brusque, weren't you?"

"Why lead him on?"

"That wasn't a marriage proposal. Just your run-of-the-mill box step."

Megan shrugged, feeling the uncomfortable pinch of the truth. Just yesterday Ingrid had lectured her on her nonexistent social life. *You have a wall around you, Megan. There's a big wide world out there beyond work. It's time you took a bite out of it.*

She'd convinced herself that being Jenny's mother was enough. The Movable Feast could fill whatever empty spaces remained inside her chest when she was alone in bed, with the sultry breeze whispering through the curtains at her window, reminding her that life was passing her by.

Before she knew it she'd be thirty, then forty, then grandmother to Jenny's children and sensual love would be a distant memory as faded as flowers in a forgotten scrapbook.

She laughed softly at the lie. Every caress, every hot wet kiss, every second of exhilarating passion that she and Jake had shared seemed as if they had happened last night.

Memory was a treacherous thing. Arguments and unpaid bills were long forgotten, but the freckle on his left shoulder blade or the way he looked at the moment when he—the memories were still there, waiting.

If only she could see him again, talk to him, be with him, burn him from her memory once and for all so she could get on with her life—

"Save me from travel agents with dancing feet." Sandy reclaimed her seat next to Megan.

Megan spun around, grateful to be pulled away from her thoughts. "That bad?"

"The worst. Someone repossessed his sense of rhythm and forgot to tell him." She sipped her crème de menthe. "Of course, there was one good thing about the experience—I got a close-up of that *gorgeous* piano player." She sighed dramatically. "Now that was one fine specimen."

"I hadn't noticed."

Sandy lowered her voice conspiratorially. "My dear, this one is hard to miss. Tall...dark...golden brown eyes to die for. And that voice! I tell you it just doesn't get much better than that boy."

An odd sensation grabbed Megan by the throat. "What about his voice?"

"Oh, you know," said Sandy, waving a hand in the air as she searched for the right words. "One of those gritty voices that manage to sound smart and sexy and savage at the same time. An Aussie, probably."

Megan glanced across the room toward the man at the piano. He sat in shadow, head down, long tapered fingers moving across the ivory keys. There was something about the curve of his neck, the pure masculine grace of his movements that made her heart feel swollen with emotion. "I wish I could see his face," she murmured.

"What about those shoulders?" mused Sandy. "I wonder if he played football."

He wasn't a brilliant piano player. His hands were too large for finesse, his movements too strong for delicacy. The softer notes of the song were trampled by his extremely male approach. Megan wondered how a man like that had managed to snare a position on the *Sea Goddess*. Unless, of course, the powers-that-be had decided every seagoing vessel needed a resident Adonis to stride among the mortals.

She knew all about Adonises. She'd married one. They didn't fare well when it came to real life. When push came to shove, they abandoned the mortal women who loved them and retreated back to Mount Olympus where they could frolic with goddesses.

*Turn around,* Megan whispered silently. *Let me see you....*

The lights went up and he turned around and what she'd been dreaming of and dreading and praying for the last six years finally happened.

Jake Lockwood was back in her life.

## Chapter Two

Sandy leaned over and touched Megan's forearm. "Are you okay?"

Megan nodded, not trusting herself to speak. All the times she had imagined seeing Jake again, all the elaborate fantasies she had entertained were nothing compared to the reality.

He slid over on the bench, making room for a flirtatious blonde with more than music on her mind. Pain, hot as the blade of a knife, sliced through her. She hated that girl for her easy grace, her laughing eyes, the fact that she sat next to the only man Megan had ever loved.

"He's gorgeous," Sandy breathed as Jake charmed the crowd gathered near the piano. "He has them eating out of his hand."

"He has that talent." Megan's voice was sharp. Clumsily she rose to her feet. "I'm leaving."

"Megan, you can't. It's early. If you don't like the music, we could—"

*This can't be happening,* she thought wildly. Things like this didn't happen in real life. Smart women didn't moon over their ex-husbands. And, even if they did, those ex-husbands didn't reappear one day out of no-where as if conjured from a dream. She needed fresh air, anything to clear her head and snap her back to reality.

She pushed through the crowd near the doorway and stepped outside. The tropical breezes caressed her like a lover's touch, intensifying the painful surge of emotion inside her chest. The only sounds were the click of her high heels on the wooden deck as she made her way aft and the hum of the ship's engine as it cut through the water. Sea spray glistened on the railing. Stacked on the starboard side, white deck chairs made gray, ghostly shapes in the darkness.

She hadn't seen him, not really. He'd been a mirage, a trick of the lighting, of years of wondering. A potent combination of brandy and loneliness. Tomorrow morning she would wake up and everything would be back to normal. Her body wouldn't ache for his. Her heart wouldn't still beat in sync with his heart.

*Go to your cabin,* a small voice whispered. *Nothing good comes of moonlight and stars and the smell of the sea.*

But she stood at the railing.

And she waited.

"Don't do this to me, Jake." Her voice broke the stillness of the endless night. "Say something."

He stepped out of the shadows and her heart seemed to stop for an instant. This was no dream. He stood before her and she understood in the deepest recesses of her soul that the power he had over her was absolute. The sea was calm but she felt as if she stood in the eye of a storm.

He was taller, broader, so perfectly male in every way that she feared she would go up in flames simply from wanting him.

"It's been a long time, Megan." Her name on his lips triggered a flood of memories.

*Open for me, Meggie...don't hold back....*

"Still beautiful," he continued, his tone light.

"You sound disappointed."

"I don't mean to." His eyes traveled the length of her body. "Growing up agrees with you."

She bridled at his words. "You might like to try it someday."

He stepped closer. She held her ground, the light of defiance in her eyes.

"You saw me in there, didn't you, Megan."

She shrugged and he caught the scent of roses on her skin. "What if I did?"

"Did you think you could avoid me for the next week?"

"Five days," she corrected him. "I was willing to give it a try."

"The ship's not that big, Megan. Sooner or later we'd have to come together."

The double entendre in his words was not lost on either of them. She gathered her shawl more tightly about her shoulders and lifted her chin. *Get ahold of yourself!* reason commanded. *Don't let him know he still has that effect on you.* She wasn't a girl any longer, naive and innocent and believing in forever after. She was a woman who'd known heartache and loss. She was the mother of a small child, *his* child, and she'd kill before she let him break her daughter's heart the way her father had broken hers.

SHE WAS DIFFERENT somehow, Jake noted as he approached her, and it wasn't just the passage of time that had brought about the changes. At twenty-five she scarcely had to worry about lines and wrinkles. Her face was as smooth as he'd remembered; her luxuriant mane of auburn hair was as shiny and full as always.

But still there was something, some indefinable element that had changed. She seemed experienced, as if the world had touched her. Changed her in ways he didn't know, would never know. He found it hard to believe she'd spent the last six years in a convent. She was a sensual, vital woman. Thinking she had turned away from the physical side of life was unfair, unreasonable, and exactly what he'd like to believe. *She's not your wife anymore, Lockwood. You have no hold on her.* If she'd taken one lover or one hundred, it was no business of his.

"It's been wonderful," she said, her words clipped. "We must do it again." She heard the tremor in her voice and silently cursed the wild emotions tearing at her heart. There was something infinitely seductive about familiarity.

He blocked her escape. "This is a small ship, Megan. We can't avoid each other."

"We can try." He was so close to her that she felt the heat of his body. He still smelled of sunshine and spice. She hadn't expected that something so insignificant would be her undoing. She wanted to bury her face against his neck and—

She tried to push past him but he grabbed her wrist, his strong fingers easily encircling it.

"Why did you run away?"

"I needed some fresh air."

"You wanted to get away from me, didn't you? Admit it, Meggie."

"Don't call me Meggie," she snapped, regaining her composure. "Nobody calls me that."

"I always called you that. From the very first."

"You don't have that right anymore." She met his eyes. "What are you doing here? Did you track me down?" Ridiculous though it sounded, she couldn't come up with a better explanation.

His eyes narrowed slightly. "What would you say if I told you I owned this ship?"

She started to laugh. "The truth never did stand in your way, did it, Jake."

"Too hard to believe I could make something of myself?"

Color flooded her cheeks and she blessed the darkness. "I didn't say that."

"You didn't have to."

"I saw you playing the piano, Jake. That's nothing to be ashamed of." Said in the precisely patronizing tones of a girl who couldn't believe she'd ever known such a person, much less have married him.

"About where you'd expect me to end up, isn't it, playing piano in a bar." There was an edge to his voice, a tone of defiance.

"This is a beautiful ship," she said, tilting her chin. "You could have done much worse."

"Yeah," he said after a moment. "I could have."

The meaning of his words was clear and instantly she found her old rich-girl persona returning full force. She should thank him for it. "I'm so pleased you've found gainful employment," she said with a toss of her head. "If I remember correctly, that used to be a problem."

Not even the darkness could hide the look of anger in his eyes. "Want to see my résumé, Meggie?"

"No, I don't want to see your résumé."

"Might find a few surprises."

"I've had enough surprises for one day, thank you." She felt giddy and disoriented, as if someone had taken her life and tilted it on its side. "Shouldn't you be getting back to your piano?"

"I'm finished for the night."

"Don't let me keep you then." She turned away from him, her heart pounding wildly inside her chest. She hadn't felt this exhilarated, this *alive,* in years. The feeling was as dangerous as it was exciting and she wanted nothing more than to run as far away from him as she could get.

"So what are you doing here, Meggie? Hard to believe Daddy's sending you out to work."

She would rather die than let him know how much this cruise meant to her. "Oh, you know how it is," she said, her tone breezy. "Even debutantes are trying their hand in the job market."

"You're here to work?"

"You don't have to sound so surprised."

"You forget who you're talking to. I'm the guy who taught you to boil water."

"Well, believe it or not, I'm trying for a franchise

with Tropicale and if you do anything to sabotage me, I'll—''

"Sabotage?'' His expression darkened into a scowl. "What the hell kind of life are you leading these days? Why would I sabotage you?''

She'd cut too close to the bone with that statement, revealing much more than she'd ever intended. Her father's treachery had left scars too deep to share with anyone. Especially not with Jake. She looked at him, memorizing the strong jaw, the powerful shoulders, that sad look in his eyes against the time when he would once again be gone. He was as rootless, as insubstantial as the Caribbean breeze, a perfect lover but no husband at all, and she would be wise to remember that.

But, dear God, he was beautiful. A fine starburst of lines radiated from the outer corners of his eyes and shadowed his smile. He looked rougher than she'd remembered, more dangerous if possible.

That was the difference. He was a man now, not the wild boy she had loved during their marriage. For a moment, she allowed herself to forget the bitterness of their divorce and drink in the masculine splendor of his lean, tanned face. Her fingers ached to trace his high cheekbones, to glide across his mouth, to outline the stubborn angles of his jaw.

Life had been kind to him these six years past and for one fierce instant she despised him for all that she'd lost.

HE SAW THE CHANGE in her instantly. Color rose to her cheeks and her eyes flashed with fire, but beneath the fire was a vulnerability that stopped him in his tracks. He'd seen that look in her eyes only one time before, when she lay beneath him as a girl on the brink of womanhood.

The level of tension between them escalated sharply and he was reminded of a sudden storm, turning the air electric with its power.

How could he have believed this encounter would be easy? He'd approached this first meeting confident that once he saw her and spoke to her, he'd realize she held no magic for him after all. *Wrong,* he thought, watching the play of starlight in her eyes. Not only was the magic still there, so were the pain and the anger and the whole messy, complicated history between them.

"Why don't we have a drink?" They needed something else to occupy them, a civilized ritual to help contain the primitive emotions that threatened to veer out of control. "Talk about old times."

"No, thank you."

The schoolmarm sound of her voice suddenly enraged him. "Grow up, Megan. It's time you played the game like an adult." They never had been very good at civilized rituals.

"You don't know what you're talking about."

"The hell I don't. I've seen your kind before, playing businesswoman while some poor lackey does all the dirty work back at the office."

"Shut up, Jake."

"It's not like that?" he asked. "You'll have to do some fast talking if you want me to buy that line."

"I don't give a damn what you buy," she snapped.

"I know who I am and what I'm doing and I don't particularly care what you think about any of it."

"Spoken like the daughter of Darrin McLean," he said with a harsh laugh. "I'll bet he's still spoiling his little princess and nailing his competition while they—"

"You bastard!" The sound of the slap bounced off the water and back at them. She began to tremble.

He grabbed her hand and held it fast. "Try it again and I hit back."

"Go to hell."

"Been there," he growled. "Want to hear about it?"

She wanted to slap him again but knew better than to try it.

He glanced down at the ring finger of her left hand.

"I'm not married," she said, noticing the direction of his gaze. "Once was more than enough."

"Neither am I."

She arched a brow. "I don't recall asking."

"You wanted to, Megan." He was back on familiar ground again, teasing, questing, hunting. "Admit it. You're as curious about me as I am about you. It's been six years. A lot can happen to a person in six years."

"You flatter yourself."

"I don't think so." He stroked the inside of her wrist with his thumb. She didn't try to move away. "There's a lot of history between us."

"Ancient history. None of it matters."

"I think it does."

"And I think you're wrong."

"Six years is a long time."

"We made a mistake and we rectified it. What's the point in rehashing the past?"

"Don't say anything," he whispered. "Just let yourself go."

He drew her into his arms. She held herself stiff as a hundred warning lights went off inside her brain. This was insane, dangerous...exciting. She caught the familiar scent of his skin, and her senses veered out of control. He cupped her chin with his hand then lowered his head toward hers.

She uttered a soft moan as he ran his tongue slowly along her lips, then eased it into her mouth, exploring the softness within. The bitterness and anger of the past temporarily vanished as a liquid sweetness flooded through her body.

His hands snaked their way up her spine and plunged into her thick hair. His hips pressed against hers and she felt his rising excitement. Her fingers were spread flat on his chest and she slid them under the smooth cotton fabric of his shirt and ran them, palms down, over his thick mat of chest hair.

His kiss moved down the side of her throat, along the slender column, to her tanned shoulder. With seductive deliberation, he nudged her lacy shawl and she let it slither down to the floor of the deck.

His burning mouth branded her shoulder, then moved slowly, inevitably, to her breast.

She cradled his silky head in her hands. With her forefingers she traced the proud curve of his cheekbones and the stubborn line of his jaw. For a moment it was as if the past six years had never happened. She was nineteen again, on fire from within for the man who had stolen her heart. She became acutely aware of her breasts, of the way her nipples grew taut as his lips moved closer. She was as warm as the tropical night and the warmth seemed to rise in waves around her, threatening to make her throw reason to the four winds.

His face was half in shadow and his sad eyes looked down into hers with a look she couldn't fathom. He couldn't hurt her any longer, so why not allow herself this one last pleasure?

Her breath caught when his fingers encircled her wrist again. His dark brows were drawn together in what looked like a scowl. She tried to pull her hand away but he held it fast.

"Jake, we can't—"

Her words turned into a muffled gasp as, with great deliberation, he separated and then kissed each one of her fingertips in turn. His mouth was hot. The scrape of his teeth against the sensitive pad of flesh was fiercely erotic. The gesture pierced her heart, catapulting her back into another time when there was only she and Jake and a wonderful future stretching before them.

Tilting her head back, she looked up at him, trying to read the expression in his eyes. The wind had picked up, whipping her hair about her face, making it as tangled and wild as her emotions. She couldn't control the rush of unwanted desire burning its way through her body.

He pulled her slightly closer with an insistent hand against the small of her back. "It was always good between us, wasn't it, Megan? Always." The simple touch of his hand against the bare flesh of her spine made her tremble with wanting him.

"Yes," she whispered, unable to deny the truth. "It was always good."

Her breasts and hips molded themselves against his body with an urgency that frightened her. She forced herself to grow rigid in his arms. He was not going to draw her close to him the way he used to do. She was older now, and smarter. Oh, he could be charming, flashing that killer smile of his, moving his powerful body with the grace of a jungle predator. Given half a chance, he could charm her right back into his bed.

"Do you remember the first time?" His voice was molten gold. "Right from the start it was good."

She struggled to dispel the magic settling around them. "I'm not interested in the past, Jake. The future is what's important to me." Jenny's future, most of all. *Dear God,* she thought, *don't let him find out about our daughter.* She had no room for him in her life, no matter that her traitorous body said otherwise.

"It was our wedding night," he went on, ignoring her protests. "They had a bucket of pink champagne on ice—"

"Pink champagne," she said with a soft laugh. "You're being kind. I doubt if a champagne grape had been anywhere near that bottle."

"So you do remember. I was beginning to wonder."

Damn him. He'd always been able to bend her to his will. "What's the point to all this? We were wonderful in the bedroom and terrible in every other room in the house.''

''There was more to our marriage than that.''

''No, there wasn't. I never knew you, Jake, not really. You were as big a mystery to me then as you are now.''

''I'm not the one who walked out on the marriage,'' he pointed out. ''You were.''

''I had good reason.'' *And you let me go without a fight.*

''I'm not arguing that, Meggie. What I'm saying is there's unfinished business between us.''

She looked away, eyes drawn to the silvery wake the *Sea Goddess* left in its path. How could she argue the point when back home their daughter slept peacefully, hugging her favorite teddy bear to her chest, dreaming dreams that Megan was determined to make come true.

''Can you deny there's something between us, Meggie?'' His voice was low, seductive…dangerous.

''No.'' She turned to face him. ''I can't. But that doesn't mean we have to act on it.''

''Maybe we should.'' He released her from his grip and her entire body yearned for his. ''Maybe that's the only way we can get rid of the past once and for all and get on with it.'' The perennial twinkle in his eyes turned darker, more intense.

''This isn't a pleasure trip for me,'' she said, her mind racing through endless winding corridors, looking for a way out. ''I'm here to work.''

''Sunday,'' he said. ''Day after tomorrow. You'll be finished by four. After that, your time is yours.''

Her eyebrows lifted. "You know about Sunday?"

"I know about everything."

She didn't doubt him. "You piano players get around."

He gave her one of those smiles that had buckled her knees back when she was young and naive. Unfortunately that smile still worked now that she was older and wiser.

"Sunday night," he said, brushing her cheek with his fingertips. "Ten o'clock." He kissed her quickly, his lips barely touching hers. Just enough to make the longing inside her grow stronger. "Right here."

"No matter what I decide?"

"No matter what you decide." The look in his eyes brooked no argument. "You owe me that much, Meggie."

She remembered the night she'd walked out on him. How she'd gone out of her way to avoid confrontation and questions and the whole unsavory business of breaking up a marriage. She hadn't known how to handle conflict or money problems or any of the thousand things that could go wrong between a husband and wife.

She simply hadn't understood that divorce only ended a marriage in the eyes of the law; it took much more than a piece of paper to convince the heart that it was over.

# Chapter Three

"Briscoe's going to be hard to beat," said Ian Macmillan, one of Jake's partners in Tropicale.

Jake looked up at him. "I wasn't that impressed."

The two men were seated in the office adjacent to the bridge. It was very late but given the charade they were playing—posing as members of the crew—this was the only time they had for executive business.

"Briscoe's the old pro of the group, best credentials this side of the cordon bleu." Macmillan laughed tiredly. "But she isn't what you'd call easy on the eyes, is she?"

Jake, who had been studying a spreadsheet of projections for the next fiscal year, grunted. "This isn't a beauty contest."

"Maybe it should be. Did you see that babe with the big green eyes?" He glanced down at the brochure Jake had kept on top of the stack of papers on the desk. "Megan McLean will have to go some length to come up with something tastier than her own sweet self."

Jake looked up. "What was that?"

"McLean," said Ian, oblivious to Jake's tone.

"Don't tell me you missed her." He held out his hand at shoulder height. "About this big." His hands described a curvy shape in the air. "Everything where it should be. Woman's got the best pair of—"

Macmillan never had a chance. Jake was on him before he finished the sentence and was about to deliver the right hook he'd perfected in the outback when a purser entered the office and pulled him off the younger man.

"What the hell's your problem?" Ian barked, rubbing his throat where Jake had grabbed him.

Jake glowered at him. "Say another word about her and, so help me, I'll—"

"I get the message," said Ian, "but the question is, why?" He forced a nervous grin. "Don't tell me you staked your claim already."

"None of your damn business." Jake reclaimed his chair.

"What's the deal, Lockwood—we got a conflict-of-interest case building here? No wonder you asked for her and not her partner."

"Just stay away from her, that's all. She's not your type."

Macmillan laughed, then rubbed his jaw again. "I haven't met one yet who isn't."

"Congratulations," Jake sneered, putting a sarcastic spin to the word. "Then this one's a first."

"I don't take orders from you, Lockwood. We're partners, remember?"

Jake knew he'd gone overboard but the feelings Megan had roused in him refused to be quieted. The thought of another man putting his hands on her made him want to punch first and ask questions later. Primitive, maybe, but effective.

"I'm wound pretty tight these days," he said by way of apology. "The *Sea Goddess* is the only woman in my life."

"You gotta get out more, Lockwood," said Ian with a relieved laugh. "I know a sweet little blonde who—"

Jake was no longer listening. He'd come close to screwing up royally and the near miss rocked him.

The thing was, he wasn't supposed to feel this way. He'd expected to want her. Desire had been a major force in their relationship and there'd been no reason to imagine its power wouldn't make itself known again.

He knew how to handle those chemical urges, how to enjoy sex but avoid involvement. What he hadn't been prepared for were these other emotions, equally strong, that were tangled up in his desire for Megan.

Anger, for one, and regret. Both of which were understandable considering the way the marriage had ended. So much left unsaid between them. So many dreams destroyed. What surprised him was the irrational sense of hope that had flared to life in the darkness.

Another man might call it love. Jake called it ridiculous.

Only one woman had ever managed to breathe life into all the hidden recesses of his soul and he'd managed to drive her away with his selfish pursuit of his own goals. Love was a thing of the past, an artifact like an arrowhead or an old tombstone.

What he was dealing with now was lust, pure and simple. Despite everything, he'd never quite gotten her out of his system and, he expected, she felt the same attraction to him.

And there was only one way to deal with it.

They needed to come together in a blaze of heat and desire, and burn away the last vestiges of their marriage. He had to find out that she was only a woman and not the elusive goddess time and fantasy had transformed her into.

Ignoring Ian's curious look, he excused himself then left the office.

"Damn it to hell," he swore as he made his way toward the dining room. He didn't want a second chance. He only wanted to put finish to whatever mysterious force it was that still tied him to her.

Why else would he be feeling guilty, pretending to be one of the crew? The idea had been for the partners in Tropicale to blend in with the other passengers, so they could hear firsthand what the passengers thought of the cruise. A clever idea and one that was extremely workable, given the more intimate size of the *Sea Goddess* when compared to a traditional cruise ship.

Yeah, it was a great idea—or, at least, it had been until he'd found himself looking into Megan's eyes and everything they'd had and lost came rushing back in on him like the tide....

*HE HADN'T WANTED to marry.*

*Only a fool would tie himself down with a wife and family when the future beckoned, all promise and glit-*

ter. He liked his freedom. He liked taking what he wanted from life, caution be damned.

Yet from that first moment on the beach when she'd looked up at him with those lazy green eyes and turned his soul to flame, he had known there were some things you didn't do with a girl like Megan McLean.

She'd been sweet in his arms and yielding, and he had little doubt he would have been able to part those shapely thighs of hers and bury himself inside her willing body.

But, damn it, it wouldn't be enough. It always had been with other women on other days, but this time he knew the rules were different. The moment he saw the flash of fire in her eyes, he'd wanted to toss her over his shoulder like one of his caveman ancestors and cart her off to his lair.

He wanted to own her. To possess her. To brand her with his touch and smell and heat until she belonged to him and him alone. The thought of another man burying himself inside her warmth made him realize he could be capable of murder.

They'd flown through the night to get to the chapel on the Las Vegas strip. Hidden beneath a blanket in the rear of the plane, he'd touched her in ways that made her shudder and it had taken a supreme act of will to keep from having her right then and there. The need in him had been that great—the dark wet heat of her body that intoxicating. He'd taken his fingers, still moist and hot from her, then rubbed them across her lips, urging her to taste herself, to know how good and sweet she would be when he found her with his mouth and tongue.

*They rode in silence to the chapel, caught up by the enormity of it all. He bought a bouquet of white roses from a sleepy clerk in the lobby. A simple gesture and an obvious one. She was used to diamonds.*

*"Oh, Jake," she whispered, burying her face in the blossoms. "They're so beautiful."*

*He wasn't a man ruled by convention. He wasn't marrying because he needed society's imprimatur on the way she made him feel; he was marrying because there was no other way to make her his own.*

*"I don't care where we live," she'd whispered later on as the door to their hotel room closed behind them. "Wherever you want to go, whatever you want to do— I don't need anything but you."*

"YOU WERE WRONG, Meggie," he said, staring out at the ocean, silvered by moonlight. She'd needed all the trappings of wealth and position that she'd known as Darrin McLean's only child.

He should have left her there on the beach where he'd found her, Daddy's little girl still as pure as the day she was born.

She'd made him want things a man shouldn't want: family, security, a house with a picket fence. To get where he wanted to be, you had to be willing to give up the things other men took for granted—and Megan hadn't been the kind of girl who'd wait around for things to get better. She was used to money and the things it could buy. Living hand-to-mouth wasn't her style.

Which was exactly what her old man had told him the first time they met. "Six months tops," Darrin

McLean said, with a look at his Rolex. "My daughter needs more than someone like you could give her."

At that moment he'd seen his sister, dying by inches in that parched cabin on that barren land, her beauty held hostage to responsibility. To poverty. Putting all of her dreams on hold while she tended house for the drunk they called a father and pretended she had all the time in the world to be happy.

Jake liked to tell himself that was the only reason he hadn't gone after her when she left, but the truth was more complex—and a hell of a lot more painful. She hadn't believed in his dreams and that fact hurt him more deeply than any left hook that had ever met his jaw.

MEGAN DOUBLE LOCKED the door to her suite that night. She wasn't sure if she was locking Jake out or herself in. Not that it mattered. Either way she was in trouble.

She tossed her evening bag on the bed and draped the shawl over the back of the boudoir chair. It slithered to the floor in a puddle of lace and she kicked it away with the pointed toe of her fancy shoe. Reaching back she tugged at the zip of her dress.

The zip refused to give. She tugged again, hard, and was rewarded with the sound of tearing fabric. "Damn," she cursed, suddenly close to tears. "Damn. Damn. Damn."

She stepped out of the dress and inspected the damage. The zipper had pulled away from the bodice and a long diagonal rip angled toward the waist. It was the last of her good dresses, the elegant designer costumes from the days when names like Dior and Versace had been as familiar as old friends.

"Okay," she said out loud, taking measure of the damage. "This isn't so bad. A good dressmaker could fix it." *Good dressmakers cost good money,* that annoying little voice inside intoned. She sank onto the bed and crushed the garment in her hands.

It was his fault. All of it. She never had trouble with zippers. Seeing Jake again after so long had turned her into a mass of nerves, incapable even of undressing herself without courting disaster. He had no business being there. Five years ago when Megan was alone with a brand-new baby and the rubble of her father's business empire falling down around her shoulders— then she would have welcomed him back into her life.

She'd been terrified and alone, wishing with all her heart that she hadn't walked out on him the first moment things got tough. Jenny was a good baby but Megan was little more than a baby herself in all the things that mattered. She needed a knight on a white charger to ride into her life and make everything right again, the way it used to be. The way it *should* be.

She'd called everywhere and everyone she could think of as she tried to find him, but Jake had vanished without a trace. She could barely manage to scrape up enough money to pay the telephone bill, much less hire a detective to track him down.

And when you came down to it, what difference would it have made? It didn't matter if he was in Paris or Cairo or Sydney. The last thing he wanted was a ready-made family and a mansion filled with bills.

"Oh, you'd love this, wouldn't you," she said as

she remembered the dangerous glitter in her ex-husband's eyes. Arrogant, spoiled Megan McLean brought to her knees. Forced to live like the common folk. She could just imagine what Jake would say if he knew she'd been living one step ahead of the bill collectors for so long that she could barely remember there was any other way.

What a wonderful joke it would be. She was sure Jake would appreciate the irony of the situation. She'd run back to the security and luxury of her father's house, only to discover that everything she'd believed in, everything she relied upon, was built on a foundation of empty promises and deceit.

Darrin McLean had kept her jewelry box filled and her wardrobe up-to-date, but when it came to keeping her safe from harm by securing her future—well, that was another story.

A framed photo of Jenny smiled at her from the nightstand. "You deserve better than that," she whispered.

Jenny deserved a father but Megan would be damned if it would be Jake Lockwood.

MEGAN AWOKE the next morning with new resolve. She was there on business and not even her ex-husband would deter her from the pursuit of her goal. The *Sea Goddess* was a big ship. There had to be room on it for both of them. She would stick to the kitchen while Jake could have the piano bar all to himself. With a little luck and some clever planning, they'd never have to see each other again.

"G'day, Meggie." He was lounging in front of the

dining room, looking tall, dark, and impossibly male. "Oversleep?"

"Shut up," she replied, a sweet smile on her face.

"They stop serving in ten minutes."

"How kind of you to give me an update."

"Must be tough traveling without a maid and butler."

"I manage," she said through clenched teeth.

She swept past him into the dining room. To her dismay he fell into step beside her. "Still not a morning person."

"How observant." She poured herself a cup of coffee from the silver urn on the sideboard. The aroma was rich and fragrant. Kona blend, she thought. Celia Briscoe was going to be tough to beat.

"The cranberry muffins are even better than the coffee," Jake said with a grin. "Makes you wonder what she'll whip up for lunch."

"Heartburn. With a double portion for you."

Jake was still laughing as he left the dining room. Amazing, she thought. He had no idea how close he'd come to death by butter knife. He'd always had the ability to punch holes in her defenses, making her conceits look foolish even to herself. At nineteen that had been nothing more than annoying. The notion that she was anything but perfect hadn't occurred to her yet. At twenty-five, however, it was a different story. She knew how it felt to fall behind in her bills, to be vulnerable to the needs of a child, to realize that no matter how hard or how well you worked, it might not be enough.

She'd come here with one goal: to nail the catering

contract with Tropicale. No matter what Ingrid said, they needed this contract to keep The Movable Feast in the black. Pretending to be rich was harder than she'd imagined. Maintaining the illusion around Jake would be difficult, but she would do it. She had no other choice.

After breakfast she changed into a bikini and joined Val and Sandy on deck. The sun was hot. The sea breeze was cool. The company was agreeable. She should have known it was too good to be true.

"G'day, ladies."

Val and Sandy snapped to attention. Megan sniffed and sank lower in her deck chair. Amazing how thick his Aussie accent got when attractive women were involved.

He towered over her, his muscular body throwing her into shadow. "G'day, Meggie."

She stretched languorously, as if she hadn't a care in the world, as if she spent every day basking in the sun. "Move, would you, Jake. You're blocking my sun."

Val, God bless her, didn't miss a beat. "Here," she said, patting the end of her deck chair. "Sit with me."

Jake favored the woman with one of his patented bad-boy grins. Megan could almost hear the hormone levels rising.

"You'll make room for me, won't you, Meggie?"

She ignored him.

He nudged her with his knee. "Shove over."

"The hell I will."

Sandy and Val stared at the two of them in open-mouthed fascination as Jake unceremoniously sat down next to her.

"Maybe we should find someplace else to sit," Sandy said with a glance toward her sister.

"You've got to be kidding," Val protested, looking from Megan to Jake then back again. "I'm not leaving until I find out what's going on."

Jake's grin widened. "You want to tell them, Meggie, or should I?"

She considered the wisdom of diving overboard and swimming back to Miami. "Jake and I were married a long time ago. It was a mercifully brief experience."

"You two were married?" Val asked, turning toward Jake.

"I threw her over my shoulder and dragged her off to Vegas to get married."

The two travel agents practically swooned.

"How romantic," Sandy cooed, turning toward Megan. "Sounds like something from a romance novel."

"He was looking for a green card," Megan snapped. "He would have married anyone with a pulse." An outright lie, but she was beyond caring. Let him worry about it.

Their eyes locked. She saw the challenge in his eyes and met that challenge with one of her own. After a moment he shrugged.

"It was fun while it lasted," he said to the two women. He turned to Meggie. "Even you have to admit that."

"No. It was many things but fun wasn't one of them." Exciting. Heartbreaking. All things in be-

tween. But not fun. The differences between them had
seen to that.

Megan's gloomy assessment of their marriage
didn't deter Val. The woman leaned across Megan and
treated Jake to an astounding expanse of cleavage.
"I've always thought Australian men were so sexy. I
mean, Mel Gibson is to die for."

"Mel Gibson is an American," Megan muttered under her breath. "He's from New York."

"But he grew up in Australia." Val waved her hand
in the air as if to brush away Megan's words. "Besides, he doesn't sound like he's from New York and
that's all that counts. He's not some dreary Wall Street
businessman."

"I know what you mean," said Sandy. "American
men are too busy making money."

Val playfully swatted Jake's arm with her magazine.
"I can't imagine you locked away in some dreary old
boardroom when there are other more interesting
rooms available."

"I'm an outdoorsman myself," Jake said, bypassing
Val's blatant invitation. "A bottle of plonk and a sailboat and I'm a happy bloke."

*One day we'll sail around the world, Meggie, just
the two of us....*

Megan lay back in her chair, closed her eyes, and
feigned indifference to the whole thing. *Don't let him
get to you like this.* She'd never survive the next four
days if she didn't get a grip on her emotions and regain
her focus.

Jake wasn't important.

Their daughter was.

It was as simple as that.

She refused to be drawn into the conversation despite Jake's best attempts and didn't relax until he went off to do whatever it was he did on the *Sea Goddess* besides play the piano and flirt with female guests.

"Excuse me for saying so," Val declared as soon as Jake was out of earshot, "but that is exactly what I've been looking for all my life."

"Be my guest," Megan shot back. "As far as I know he's footloose and fancy-free."

Val leaned forward. "You wouldn't mind?"

She waved her hand in the air. "I haven't seen Jake since the day I walked out on him. If you want a shipboard wedding, it's fine with me. I'll be your maid of honor."

"I don't know about the wedding," Val said, "but I sure wouldn't mind a wedding *night.*"

*ONE HOUR AFTER they arrived in Las Vegas, Megan and Jake were married at Sweet Sue's Wedding Chapel. Two strangers stood up for them as part of the one-hundred-fifty-dollar matrimonial package that included a room for the happy couple.*

*The Silver Dollar Hotel catered to people with big dreams and small budgets. Positioned between the Little House of Matrimony and Sweet Sue's, it offered king-size water beds, complimentary pink champagne, and a place to be alone.*

*"Room 775." The bellman swung open the door and ushered them into the room. "Champagne's on*

*ice, the bathroom's through that door, and you got a great view of the Strip.''*

Megan turned away as Jake reached into his pocket for some change. She tried not to notice the stained carpeting or the threadbare bedspread or the faint but unmistakable smell of cigar smoke in the air. All her life she'd dreamed about her wedding night. The room would be lit by fat pink candles that smelled of gardenias. Soft music, Dom Pérignon, a wide bed with sheets of the finest percale with lace-trimmed hems.

She'd never imagined anything like this...this wreck of a place. It doesn't matter, she told herself. All that matters is Jake. *They could have waited. She could have had the wedding of her dreams. She was naive enough to still believe her father would come around and accept Jake as a son-in-law.*

*But Jake was a proud man and an impatient one and she'd known beyond a doubt that she had to grab hold of him before he disappeared on his way to some new adventure, taking her chance for happiness with him.*

The door closed behind the bellman. She held her breath as Jake crossed the room toward her. Desire, fierce and sweet, rose up inside her and she turned toward him and for a moment she forgot the carpet and the bedspread and the fact that they didn't have a chance in the world to make their marriage work and she went to him for the first time as his wife.

''I can't give you the things you're used to,'' he said as he swept her into his arms.

''I don't care,'' she whispered. ''You're all that I want. You're all that I need.''

*Afterward they lay together in the afterglow of lovemaking. Megan had never felt closer to anyone in her life. The act of joining their bodies had also joined their souls and she longed to know everything about the man who was now her husband.*

*"You know everything there is to know about me,"* she said, propping herself up on her elbows and looking at him. *"All I know is that you're twenty-five years old, from Australia, and never been married."*

*He pulled her down until she lay across his chest. "That's all you need to know." His big rough hands caressed the small of her back, cupped her buttocks.*

*"But I want to know all about your family, Jake."* She giggled as she tried to squirm out of his grasp but he held her fast. *"I'm a Lockwood now, too."*

*His grip on her tightened. An older, more experienced woman might have recognized the signs but Megan was too young and too besotted to care.*

*"I have an older sister in Queensland."*

*She waited. "And?"*

*"My parents are dead," he snapped. "I barely knew my mother. I might as well have never met my father." Two years dead that month and unlamented.*

*"Oh, Jake." Her voice went soft and her eyes brimmed with tears. "You must miss him so much—"*

*"I don't want to talk about them." He lifted her hips until she was poised over him. "I don't want to talk at all."*

*It was hard to keep her mind on anything but his power and heat. "Wh-what's your sister's name?"*

*"Shut up, Meggie."*

*"But they're my family too."*

*"Forget them."*

*"But I—"*

*He lowered her slowly, steadily, onto his erection and she melted around him. There would be plenty of time to learn all about his family...a lifetime.*

SOMEHOW SHE MADE IT through lunch. Celia Briscoe served up a magnificent southwestern feast and Megan had to work hard to hang on to her self-confidence. To her surprise Jake was seated at the head table. His rumbling laugh, sensual and unmistakable, awakened another set of memories that she would rather leave buried. Once he met her eyes across the dining room and she felt as if he held her in his arms.

She'd fallen for his charm years ago, but now the last thing she wanted was to be diverted from the task at hand: securing a permanent position for The Movable Feast. She'd worked too hard for too many years to allow it to slip away in a haze of sexual passion.

Desire—that was all that it was. She was certain of it. If she'd lived six years without chocolate, no doubt she'd be entertaining fantasies of a Hershey bar that were every bit as voluptuous and enticing as her fantasies about Jake.

Logic, however, didn't render those fantasies any less potent. She found herself replaying their moonlight encounter again and again until she was weak with longing.

She glanced again across the room. A petite blonde fluttered around him like a pheromone-crazed butterfly. Maybe she hadn't been that far off the mark when she'd wondered if he'd been hired as the resident

Adonis. She had to admit he added a certain rough-hewn male sex appeal to the exquisitely appointed yacht. With his movie-star good looks and renegade soul, he could probably have any woman he wanted just by crooking his little finger.

*But he wants you.*

Last night he'd made it crystal clear that she still had the power to make him want her. They both recognized that not even time had diminished the primal attraction between them. Try as she might to banish the memory of his kisses, she could still taste him on her lips. Sweet and dangerous and impossible to resist.

She pushed back her chair and rose to her feet. Val, Sandy and her other luncheon companions looked up at her. "If you'll excuse me, I think I'll go back to my cabin and do some work on my menu plan."

The moment after she closed the cabin door behind her, she dialed Ingrid's number. She needed to connect with home, to be reminded of everything that was really important in her life.

"Details!" Ingrid demanded the second Megan said hello. "Tell me about the suite, the weather, the men...."

Megan laughed, feeling her real world move back into focus. "Gorgeous, perfect...interesting."

"You can do better than that."

"Is Jenny there?"

"She's playing Barbie with Stace."

"I'm dying to hear her voice."

"Give me some juicy details then I'll let you speak to your daughter."

*Jenny's father works on the ship, Ingrid. I feel like*

*I'm nineteen years old again and it scares the hell out of me.* "You wouldn't believe this suite," she said instead. "Mahogany paneling, gilt faucets, a mirror over the bed—"

"A what!"

"Just seeing if you were paying attention, Ingrid."

"Too bad," Ingrid shot back. "If you remember, I told you to have fun."

"And if *you* remember, I told you I'm here on business."

"Only until tomorrow night. Monday and Tuesday are pure R & R. If you don't come home with a tan and a smile on your face, you're no partner of mine."

"I'll be smiling if I come back with a contract."

"There's more to life than business."

"I know," said Megan, remembering the way Jake had looked in the moonlight. She launched into a lively description of her cabin, right down to the paneled wall near the bathroom that supposedly concealed a secret passageway that linked various suites.

"How wonderfully decadent," Ingrid cooed. She named the billionaire who had first owned the yacht. "No wonder he always looked so tired. The man never slept."

"This phone call is costing us a small fortune," Megan declared. "Let me say hi to Jenny and I'll hang up."

A moment later her daughter's sweet voice curled itself inside Megan's ear. "We're having pizza tonight. Can I have pepperoni on mine?"

"That's up to Ingrid, sweetheart."

"And ice cream for dessert?"

"Ask Ingrid," Megan said with a laugh. "She's in charge while I'm away."

Jenny chattered on about the class trip she'd taken that day and Megan found her eyes filling with sentimental tears as Jenny described the glass-bottom boat and all the wonders she'd seen beneath the sea. Megan could just imagine her little girl's round cheeks all pink from the sun, her big, golden brown eyes glittering with excitement. Jenny was a small, volatile bundle of energy and enthusiasm, so much her father's daughter that at times it almost hurt Megan to look at her.

*If only I could be sure I was doing the right thing for you, Jenny,* she thought, *but I'm as new at this as you are.* There were times she felt as if she were running just one step ahead of her little girl, trying desperately to pave the way for her.

"Do you have your four-leaf clover, Mommy?" Jenny asked in her piping voice.

"Absolutely," Megan answered solemnly, touching the charm that hung from the chain around her neck. "I'll keep it with me every second."

"It'll bring you good luck."

"I have you," said Megan, wishing she could envelop her daughter in a bear hug. "How lucky can one woman be?" Her marriage may have been a failure, but out of that painful interlude had come something truly precious, this little girl who meant everything to her.

"You'll be home for my birthday?"

"Absolutely," said Megan. "Do you think I'd miss the most important day of the year?"

"Don't forget to send me postcards, Mommy."

"I promise. A postcard from every port."

"Send me a postcard, too," Ingrid added as she returned to the phone. "Tell me you enjoyed at least one moonlight kiss."

"Not interested," she said lightly. She had found out last night what dangers lurked in moonlight kisses.

"If I weren't nine months pregnant, I'd trade places with you."

"You wouldn't trade places with anyone and you know it, Ingrid."

The stab of envy, sharp and unexpected, lingered after they'd said goodbye. For all of Ingrid's grumbling about her second pregnancy, one fact was very clear: Ingrid loved her children and her husband, and was lucky enough to be loved in return.

Neither Megan's privileged childhood nor her promising future could compare with that.

She set up her laptop computer on the lacquered desk, and spent a few hours poring over the plans for floral arrangements and table designs. She would have loved the opportunity to acquaint herself with the galley below deck but it was off-limits until tomorrow morning when she began her audition. Celia Briscoe had outdone herself today and Megan could feel the pressure building.

She massaged her temples, wishing she'd remembered to bring aspirin with her. It had been too easy, she thought, resting her head on the desk as the ship rocked gently. The anger between her and Jake had flared to life again with the quick intensity of a brushfire. So had the sexual attraction; it burned away the barriers between them with its ferocious heat. Like a force of nature, that chemistry between them had been there from the first. Divorce hadn't dampened the fire—and neither had time.

She was so tired of only living half a life. Being Jenny's mother was a joy and her career brought her a great deal of pleasure. But there was a part of her that had been ignored for far too long. She needed to feel like a woman again. It was as if the deeply sensual and sexual part of her nature had been locked away with her divorce papers, vanished along with the man who had once been her husband and lover.

Maybe Jake was right. Maybe the only way to break free of the past was to burn it away in a blaze of passion. Give in to the lure of sultry night breezes and soft whispers and ancient promises of pleasure. She wasn't a girl any longer. She knew that life was seldom easy and often unfair. She'd left the last of her illusions behind the day her father died and she became yesterday's news, forgotten the moment her gold card was canceled and her bank accounts picked clean by hungry creditors.

Still she had managed to hold her head high and forge a new life for herself and her little girl. A life based on respect and honesty and hard work. She'd learned how to function on her own, how to rely upon nobody but herself. And she would teach Jenny to be self-reliant if it was the last thing she ever did.

But there were still too many questions left unresolved. Too many emotions tugging at her heart, keeping her rooted in the past when she longed to run free.

Was she mad to believe that she could offer herself up to the inferno and walk away unscathed?

SUNDAY MORNING SHE ROSE before the alarm, then threw herself into her chores with single-minded determination.

Breakfast, lunch, afternoon tea, all went off without a hitch. Compliments flowed as freely as champagne at the open bar near the pool.

But not even the fact that the franchise with Tropicale now seemed within her grasp was enough to cool the fire inside that grew hotter as ten o'clock approached.

Sandy and Val greeted her as she entered the bar.

"Will you look at that dress!" Sandy fanned herself. "Talk about hot." She turned to Val. "Can you believe this is the same flour-speckled wretch who was slaving away in the galley all day?"

"The wonders of makeup," said Megan, forcing a smile.

Val stepped closer to Megan as her sister drifted off into the crowd gathered around the piano. "Are you seeing him tonight?"

Megan's smile faltered. "Excuse me?"

Val touched her arm lightly. "Don't look at me like that, Megan. I was only teasing."

"Sorry. It's been a long day. I guess I'm a little short-tempered."

"He's standing near the bar," Val said, a half smile on her face. "What I wouldn't give for five minutes alone in a dark room with that gorgeous specimen...."

He was dressed all in black. It seemed to Megan as

if the darker forces of the night were gathered in his eyes as his gaze met hers. The thundering of her heart all but drowned out the soft music and the low buzz of conversation.

The corners of his mouth quirked upward. She knew that smile intimately. Half invitation, half wry amusement. The same odd combination that had kept her off balance throughout their marriage.

Maybe this wasn't such a terrific idea after all. They'd been divorced for years. She'd made a life without him. She didn't need him. She didn't love him. But, dear God, how very much she wanted him....

She stepped outside, seeking the cover of darkness.

He was next to her in an instant. "We need to talk."

She nodded. "Yes."

He slipped a large hand under her elbow and led her toward a pair of deck chairs in the corner. If she'd expected him to claim the adjacent chair, she was sorely mistaken. His thigh brushed hers as he sat down next to her and it was all she could do to keep from running for her life.

A hot flush rose up from her breasts, over her throat, and across her cheeks.

"We have some unfinished business, Megan."

"I know."

At the very least he'd expected a coy laugh or polite demurral. He got neither. Those beautiful green eyes of hers met his head-on. There was a flinty strength in the set of her chin that had nothing to do with the spoiled-little-rich-girl behavior he'd known during their marriage. She knew what he was about and she'd made her decision.

She lowered her eyes and looked away for a moment, an odd note of submission in a woman as fiercely independent as his ex-wife now seemed to be. Again he caught that look of vulnerability, the sense that all was not as it seemed. Her lashes fluttered briefly against the curve of her cheekbones and when she met his eyes again he knew exactly what she had decided.

"What are your plans for tomorrow?"

"Sleeping late." She didn't trust her voice to say more.

"We dock around eleven tomorrow morning for the beach party." He looked into her eyes. "You'll meet me at the gangway at eleven-thirty."

"I don't think—"

He placed a finger against her lips and she shivered at his touch. This was her one chance, maybe her only chance, to relegate Jake to memory.

"Don't think," he whispered. "Thinking always got us in trouble." He brushed her chin with his hand. "Be there, Megan. Give us one day for old times' sake."

Their gazes locked. Once again his eyes held a challenge. One day, she thought. Twenty-four hours to put the past to rest and get on with living.

Maybe the way to reclaim her soul was to give him her body. Maybe if she discovered once and for all that he was only a man, no different than any other man, she would finally be free.

"Yes," she said at last. "I'll be there."

## Chapter Four

"Do you know what time it is, Megan?" Ingrid's voice, heavy with sleep, crackled through the phone line.

"Late," said Megan apologetically. "You know I wouldn't call if it wasn't important."

"You already told me you aced the assignment," Ingrid said through a yawn. "Don't tell me they've offered us the franchise already."

"It's nothing to do with business. Jake's here."

There was a long silence from Ingrid. Then, "Jake as in Jake-your-ex-husband?"

"That's the one."

"You're kidding me, aren't you?"

"He's here, Ingrid. He works on the ship."

"Omigod. How...what is he—"

"I don't know. All I know is that he's here in the flesh." The gorgeous, incredible, *dangerous* flesh.

"The ship's not that big. Where has he been hiding?"

"He hasn't been hiding. I met him the first night."

"And you didn't tell me?"

"I had other things to think about, Ingrid." Winning the franchise, for one.

"Did you tell him about Jenny?"

"Absolutely not!"

"Don't you think you should?"

"Jenny is none of his business," Megan stated firmly. "She belongs to me."

"He's her father."

"Only biologically."

"That's usually more than enough to qualify."

"Not in this case."

"Look," said Ingrid, "we're doing fine without the Tropicale franchise. If you want to take the next plane home I'll understand."

"Why would I take the next plane home?" Megan asked, bristling. "Let him go home." Wherever that might be. "I'm here to work."

"You've done your work." Ingrid paused a beat. "You're not thinking of—"

"What if I am?"

"You've got it all wrong, Megan. You have a fling with someone *new,* not with your ex-husband."

"I know what I'm doing."

"I don't think you do."

"Is Jenny okay?"

"You're changing the subject."

"Is she okay?"

"She's asleep."

"Don't tell her about Jake."

"Of course not!" Ingrid sounded horrified. "That's none of my business."

Megan laughed. "That's the first time I've ever heard you say that, Ingrid."

"Be careful," Ingrid warned, her voice filled with concern. "Don't think ex-husbands can't break your heart just as easily the second time around."

"Trust me," said Megan. "My heart is safe."

She hung up the telephone, her words ringing in her ears.

Standing out there in the moonlight, it had made perfect sense. Fight fire with fire. The way to break Jake's sensual hold over her life was to give in to temptation and finally write Finished to a marriage that should never have been.

*But what about Jenny?* She owed it to Jake to tell him that he had a beautiful five-year-old daughter. But she also owed it to her daughter to keep her safe from heartache. She'd loved her own father with her whole heart and he'd taken that love and used it against her to further his own purposes. No one would ever do that to Jenny.

Her hand went to the four-leaf clover charm that dangled at the base of her throat. Jenny had saved up her allowance for months in order to buy that charm for Megan and it meant more to her than the pearl chokers and trips to Paris that had been part and parcel of her own girlhood. "You're the best mommy in the whole world," Jenny had said, flinging her arms around Megan's neck.

*Not yet,* thought Megan, eyes filling with tears, *but I'm working on it.*

"McLean did a damn good job," declared Ian Macmillan. "I didn't know The Movable Feast would finish that strong."

"I agree," said Jake. They were in his office, holding their late-night meeting. "She bested Celia Briscoe. Walters will have to go some."

"Did you see the way she had the crew eating out
of her hand? Even Crowley gave one hundred per-
cent."

Jake grunted something noncommittal. Last night
he'd exposed too much to his associate. He wasn't
about to make that mistake again. The truth was, Megan had dazzled everybody with her abilities. He
found it difficult to equate the spoiled brat he'd been
married to with the accomplished woman he'd
watched perform today.

Ian was waxing enthusiastic about the innovative
way Megan had decorated the alfresco dining area.
Jake nodded and kept his attention focused on the
spreadsheets on his desk.

She'd always been beautiful. Now she was accomplished as well. He wanted to know what had brought
about the change.

"Look," he said, stifling a fake yawn. "Why don't
we call it a night and pick it up again same time tomorrow?"

"You forget something?" Macmillan countered.
"We're meeting Haines and Ogilvie on La Mirada tomorrow morning for an update."

Jake swore softly. "Count me out."

"The hell I will. Haines is the money man. You
don't say no to the money man."

"Try me." He'd waited too long for the chance to show Megan who and what he had become.

"Hey," said Macmillan, looking aggrieved, "we've come this far, Lockwood. Don't blow it now."

They both knew that the Tropicale corporation was a volatile mixture of personalities and bank accounts. All it would take was the touch of a match to blow it all sky-high.

"Damn it to hell," he swore, flinging his pen against the wall. "I'll be there. But let's make it early."

Macmillan beat a quick exit. Smart man. Jake's moods were legendary.

As president of Tropicale, he couldn't renege on his associates. Businesses weren't built that way. Even rebels couldn't get away with shortchanging their partners. He'd worked long and hard to build a company that would reflect the way he believed a business should be run—blowing off the meeting with Haines and the other money men wasn't part of it.

But, damn it, neither was giving up his one chance to burn Megan from his memory forever.

He reached for the room phone. He could call her and let her know. Maybe reschedule their rendezvous for the next day in St. Denis. He put the phone back down. Not good enough. He needed to see her, smell her, touch her. *So walk down to her suite and tell her.* He paced the room like a caged wildcat. That was the simplest, easiest way to remedy it. *Yeah, but what if someone sees you standing in front of her door?* He'd not only blow her reputation, he'd undermine Tropicale as well. His eye was caught and held by the ornate carving on the paneled wall behind his bed. A grin tilted the ends of his mouth.

There was another way, however, and no one would ever know....

CANDLELIGHT. WINE. A bubble bath.

Megan sank deeper into the marble tub. Jasmine-scented bubbles tickled the underside of her chin while soft music floated in from the bedroom.

Why did people take showers, she mused, raising a lazy arm toward the ceiling and watching drops of water slide back down her arm. Showers were so impersonal, so *quick.*

Bubble baths, however, were intimate, time-consuming, decadent and sensual—everything you could possibly want. She couldn't remember the last time she had felt so deeply relaxed.

Of course, the fact that she was luxuriating in a bathtub built for two hadn't escaped her.

"Who needs company?" she murmured, leaning back and floating to the other side of the tub. All you needed was a good imagination and a stockpile of romantic fantasies and a woman could get along just fine.

She chuckled as she thought of the beautifully produced book of lore she'd found on the nightstand next to her bed. Tropicale had obligingly gathered up all of the extant romantic stories about the *Sea Goddess* and offered them up for delectable bedside reading.

Apparently the hidden corridors and passageways that linked various suites had seen more traffic over the years than Interstate 80. Her own suite had once been occupied by a European princess who'd carried on a steamy liaison with a sultan who'd commandeered three cabins aft.

She could imagine the excitement of it all, heart pounding in anticipation, knowing that any second the secret panel would slide open and you'd be swept up into passion and— What was that sound? It seemed to come from the hallway, a soft rat-a-tat against the wall.

She sat up straight in the tub. There it was again. Definitely a tapping sound. She reached for the king-size bath sheet draped over the warming rack and stepped from the tub. Creaking pipes, more than likely. She padded into the hallway, leaving wet footprints behind. It would be great fun to think the ghost of some romantic fool still walked the passageways, but she was far too much of a realist to entertain that notion for long.

"Megan."

She jumped, clutching the towel to her breasts. "I didn't hear that," she vowed, heart pounding.

"Megan, open up."

She didn't hear that, either.

Cautiously she stepped closer to the outer wall. "Who's there?"

"Jake. We need to talk."

"I don't know how to open walls. Why don't you knock on the door like a normal person?"

"There's a latch at two o'clock on the sunburst carving in the middle of the left panel."

She hesitated. What was the difference, really, if he came in through the wall, the window, or the door?

She flipped the latch, then stepped back. The wood creaked, then she watched as part of the wall slid open and Jake stepped into the room.

"You always did know how to make an entrance," she said as he slid the wall closed behind him. "Did you ever consider using the phone?"

He was staring at her as if he'd never seen her before. "Some things have to be done in person."

"Jake!" Her voice was sharp. "Don't look at me like that."

"Can't help it, Meggie. I wasn't expecting to see so much of you."

She followed his line of vision, then pulled the towel up toward the base of her throat. "And I wasn't expecting to see you at all."

His gaze traveled the length of her body. She could almost feel the sizzle against her wet skin. She was tempted to make a dash for the bathroom and slam shut the door behind her but she stood her ground.

"You interrupted my bath," she said, meeting his eyes.

"Don't let me stop you." He looked altogether too pleased with himself.

"You've already done that." Again she adjusted the towel. "What do you want, Jake?"

He was finding it tough to think. Her skin glistened in the low light of the hallway, droplets of water slithering over the tops of her breasts, disappearing into the shadowy cleavage barely covered by the towel. He wanted to follow their progress with his tongue.

"About tomorrow," he said. "I have to cancel."

"Fine," Megan replied, her tone bright and false. "No problem."

"You don't understand. I have to meet somebody in town."

"I'm sure you do," she said smoothly. "Don't let me stop you."

"Damn it, Megan. It's business." He stopped short of telling her he was one of Tropicale's major partners.

"You don't have to explain anything to me, Jake." She turned away from him, her soft fall of hair obscuring her face.

He reached for her arm. Her skin was soft beneath his hand. Silky. Warm as a tropical breeze.

Megan met his eyes. It was only a hand on her arm. Yet that simple touch was her undoing.

"You planned this." It was a statement of fact. Not an accusation.

"No," he said. "Not this."

His words reached her as if from a great distance. She felt as if the power of the ocean were gathered inside her chest, its relentless roar drowning out the little voice that tried to tell her it wasn't too late to stop this madness.

He moved closer...or did she? Not that it mattered. Somehow her back was pressed against the cool wood paneling, her breasts crushed against the warm wall of his chest, her fingers laced behind his neck.

She felt poised on top of a giant roller coaster, ready to swoop down to earth, then rush up again with nothing holding her safely in the seat. It was a feeling of reckless excitement, coupled with the sweetness of fa-

miliarity, that made her feel more alive than she had
for a very long time.

A sense of inevitability filled the room like a third
presence.

He placed his hands low on her hips, guiding her
even closer to him. He nuzzled the base of her throat;
his tongue flicked across the sensitive spot, causing
her mind to spiral upward like a helium-filled balloon.
Nothing in her life had ever seemed as good, as right,
as being in his arms at this moment.

His hands moved along her shoulders, thumbs meeting at the soft hollow of her throat. She shivered with
delight as his mouth slanted over hers.

It was an act of possession.

To hell with sanity, to hell with past bitterness. She
wanted him more than she'd wanted anything in her
life.

This was coming home.

A wild ride into the unknown with the only man
she'd ever loved.

"Megan?" His voice was half growl, half caress.

She nodded. With one sure move he swept her up
into his arms. The towel slipped away from her body
and she reached for it.

"No," he said. "You won't be needing that."

She was naked in his arms, her mind emptied of all
but the sensual feel of his body against hers, of his
strength and warmth. She looped her arms around his
neck and pressed her face against his. The smell of his
skin, the faint shadow of his beard against the strong
curve of his jaw—she closed her eyes against a diz-

zying rush of sensation that threatened to steal away what remained of her sanity.

She was lighter than a dream in his arms as he carried her to the bedroom, yet the power she had over him was absolute. Her body was still warm from her bath, her skin moist and fragrant. He laid her down on the bed, her mane of auburn hair fanning across the pillow like living fire. She reached for the ivory satin duvet but he swept it to the floor with one swift movement of his hand.

"Jake," she whispered, "this isn't fair...."

He kicked off his shoes, then reached for the button on his pants. "I'll make it fair."

A wildfire raged inside his gut as he stripped off his clothes then joined her on the bed. It would be easy to part her thighs and bury himself inside her, taking what she offered again and again until the flames were nothing more than embers. He wanted it fast and he wanted it now, a furious mating of male and female, but there was something about the look in her wide green eyes, the rapid sound of her breathing in the quiet room, that made him reconsider.

He leaned up on one elbow and let his gaze travel the length of her body. She was as slim as he'd remembered, as firm and sweet, but there was something different. A certain lushness, a womanly roundness to her curves that reminded him she wasn't a girl any longer.

Slowly he brought his hand to rest on the curve of her hip. His palm registered her warmth, the silky feel of her skin, the way she trembled slightly at his touch.

Not with fear, he knew. With need. The same need that sent heat flowing through his veins.

She reached for him but he shook his head.

"Not yet," he said, his voice gruff with desire. "Not if you want it to last."

She laughed low in her throat. He wondered how many other men had heard her laugh like that. A primitive rage battled with lust. He hated the other men who had known her body. He wanted to burn their memory from her brain, brand her with his mouth, his hands, until she regretted the day she'd walked out the door.

Swiftly he moved to the foot of the bed.

"Every part of you," he said, encircling her ankle with his hand. "Every inch...."

Her back arched and she moaned as he drew his tongue along the rise of her instep. Slow and hot and wet enough to remind her that she was a flesh-and-blood woman and that he was a hungry man.

"Turn over," he said, his hands moving toward her knees. He felt her stiffen with alarm and he pressed his mouth to the inside of her knee. "Trust me, sweetheart...."

She shouldn't. He was a stranger to her. She knew nothing about the last six years of his life and, dear God, there was so much about her that he couldn't even imagine.

But his hands were so strong and warm against the tender flesh at the tops of her thighs and it had been so long since she'd felt like a woman.

She moved as if in a dream. The percale sheets felt cool against her belly and breasts and she pressed her face into the pillow, her pulse hammering in her ears, all but drowning out her soft inarticulate cries.

He was a magic man, a conjurer of fantasies. He brought her to aching life each place he touched. Calves...the backs of her knees...the rounded swell of her buttocks.

"Lift up, Meggie," he whispered, his mouth pressed against her shoulder. "Slide this pillow under you."

She felt wickedly sensual, wild with desire, as his lips found the sensitive base of her spine.

"Oh God," she moaned, "Jake...."

He slid his hands beneath her thighs, then found her with his fingertips. His touch was light at first, an insinuation. She moved restlessly against him, her blood sounding a call older than the stars.

Her heat, her smell, the sound of her cries were pushing him to the end of madness.

He rolled her onto her back. "Hang on, Meggie. This is one ride we're taking together."

But first there was something he needed to take care of. For both of them.

Moments later she opened to him. Her excitement matched his own. He lowered himself slowly, testing his self-control, until he was poised against her heat. Her fingernails raked his buttocks. "Now...." Her voice was high, her tone urgent.

She welcomed him, drawing him more deeply into her body than he would have imagined possible. She was tight and hot, her muscles working in tiny, mind-shattering contractions around him.

He was gathering speed, climbing faster and faster,

moving inexorably toward the release his body demanded.

"Open your eyes, Meggie. I want to watch you when it happens."

She knew it was wrong, that it was dangerous, that nothing would ever be the same again, but a thrill of dark pleasure rippled through her body at his words. At that moment she would have done anything he asked. He was her only reality, her only safety.

She let her hands slide along the sinewy muscles of his arms, feeling his veins, rich with blood, beneath her fingertips.

"Ride with me, Meggie," he urged. "We're almost there...."

The fire grew hotter. She could see the flames. Feel them pulling her toward the inferno.

She wrapped her legs around his hips as he pinned her arms over her head. Sweet bondage...then even sweeter release.

Megan shuddered around him. He was part of her, could feel what she felt, even as his own climax exploded. Her pleasure was deep, shattering—he saw it in the startled look in her wide green eyes, the high color in her cheeks, the way her full lips parted. Nothing in his life, no experience, no fantasy, came close to the primitive thrill he found watching the woman he'd once loved find paradise in his arms.

## Chapter Five

Jake was the first to break the silence. "We always were good together."

She couldn't deny it. Not with her body flushed and damp with passion, with him still inside her. "Were you surprised?"

He moved against her, his laughter low. "Gratified."

"This doesn't mean anything, Jake," she warned. "It was just this once."

"For old times' sake."

"Something like that."

"Nothing more?"

"I don't still love you," she said bluntly, "if that's what you're implying."

"Love's never had much of anything to do with what happens between us."

His words stung and she found herself blinking away sudden and embarrassing tears. "Then we both understand what this is about."

"Settling old scores?"

She looked at him. *I did love you once, Jake. I was just too young and selfish to know what it meant.*

"Putting the past behind us," she answered after a moment.

"Some people might say it's the same thing."

There was something in the tone of his voice, a certain ironic spin that sent a small frisson of alarm up her spine. "I know the difference between sexual chemistry and love, Jake."

An odd smile crossed his face. "And this was...?"

"Sex," she said, her tone sharp. "Animal magnetism. Anything you want to call it."

He moved away from her until they were no longer joined, then leaned back against the headboard. "Good," he said after a moment. "I'm glad we understand each other."

"Good," she repeated, tugging the sheet up under her chin. "Not that there was ever any doubt."

"Just because two people are great in the sack is no reason to pretend they can make a marriage work."

"Only a fool would think that."

"That's where we went wrong the last time. We should have had an affair."

"Marriage was a ridiculous idea," Megan agreed, feeling unreasonably sad. "Everyone said so."

He met her eyes. "Especially your father."

"I don't want to talk about my father."

He rubbed the cheek she'd slapped during their first encounter on deck. "I seem to remember something to that effect."

"I'm sorry," she said stiffly. "I shouldn't have hit you."

"So what's your old man up to these days?"

"I said I don't want to talk about him."

"He must hate seeing his little princess out there mingling with the commoners."

"Jake—" Her voice held a warning.

He ignored it. "Come on, Meggie. I'd be lying if I pretended I gave a damn about the pommy bastard. I bet he still hates me as much as I—"

"He's dead." The words hung there in the air between them.

"I get the message," he said, not getting it at all. "I'll back off."

She forced herself to meet his eyes. "My father is dead, Jake."

His expression didn't change but she heard his slow intake of breath. "When did he—"

"Five and a half years ago."

"Heart attack?"

Dangerous territory. "He drowned."

"Darrin McLean? Your dad won a silver medal at the '56 Olympics."

Holding the sheet to her breasts, she swung her legs from the bed. "I don't want to talk about this anymore." She started for the bathroom.

He reached across the bed and grabbed her wrist. "Megan...."

She tried to pull away from him but he held her fast. "Don't tell me you're sorry because I won't believe you. You hated my father."

"And he hated me." His grip on her wrist tightened. "I am sorry, Meggie. For you. Your old man was an arrogant, selfish SOB but he had one redeeming feature—he loved you more than anything in the world."

She thought she would die from the pain that gripped her heart. There was one thing Darrin McLean had loved more than his daughter and that was his own comfort. But she would rather walk barefoot on hot coals than tell Jake the truth.

Tears burned behind her lids and she looked away.

"Meggie?" His voice was uncharacteristically gentle. "I don't want to hurt you."

She shook her head. "You didn't. It's just—" Just what? All she could offer him was a lie because the truth was still too devastating for her to comprehend.

Clumsily he stroked her hair. "He was a tough act to live up to," he said. "I would've sold my soul to be able to take care of you the way he did."

"He was my hero," she added, voice breaking. "I thought he would live forever."

He was quiet, thinking of the despair she must have felt when McLean died. "You should've called me. You shouldn't have gone through it alone."

She fell silent but the look on her face spoke volumes.

"I guess a piano player wouldn't have fit in with that crowd, would it, Meggie?"

"I didn't say that."

"No," he admitted, "you didn't. But you're not denying it." He could imagine the scene after McLean's death; his cronies must have gathered around Megan like vultures around a corpse.

She straightened her shoulders, tilted that stubborn chin. "What could you have done for me if I had called you, Jake? It's not like you'd know how to handle the situation."

*Now's the time, Lockwood.* The piano player owned the company and the yacht and more fabulous things than she'd ever dreamed of. If he was looking for shock value, she'd handed him the opportunity of a lifetime.

But the words wouldn't come. There was something about the look in her eyes, the oddly affecting set of her mouth that kept him from knocking her back with the truth.

She drew the sheet more tightly around her. "We were idiots to think going to bed together would make a difference."

He stroked her wrist with his thumb. "Maybe we didn't do it right."

She laughed despite herself. "It doesn't get much more right than that, Jake."

"Maybe it wasn't as good as we thought it was."

"Sleight of hand."

"An illusion?"

He released his grip on her wrist. She didn't move away. Rising from the bed he drew her into his arms.

Megan knew it was as crazy as it was dangerous. That this was the last place she should be.

That she couldn't turn away from him. Not for anything on earth.

"God, Meggie...." His large thumbs moved across her nipples and she bit the inside of her lip to keep from crying out. He lowered his head. His dark hair was cool and silky against her skin, his mouth hot as he encircled her nipple.

She arched against him, fingers threaded through his hair. Before they had come together in heat. The heat was still there, and the passion, but there was something else between them now. Something she couldn't put a name to but recognized in the way her body responded to him, in the way she wished this moment never had to end.

Suddenly it struck her as a terrible waste that she knew so little about the man who had been her husband.

He'd seemed dangerous to her at nineteen, as wildly powerful as a force of nature and just as unpredictable. He was filled with ideas, crazy schemes to make a million dollars. She'd never wanted for anything in her life and his ambition made her feel as if she should apologize for having the good fortune to be born rich.

What a shame it was that understanding had come too late to do them any good.

Not that it mattered. This wasn't about renewal. It was about putting the past behind her and building a new life, a life with a man who would be a husband to her—and a father to Jenny.

Two things Jake Lockwood could never be.

MEGAN OPENED HER EYES to find herself alone in bed.

"Jake?" She raised up on one elbow and smothered a yawn.

"Don't get up." He stood near the open porthole, naked except for a pair of jeans that rode low on his hips. "It's not even dawn yet."

The sight of him, splendid and male, in the shadowy blue light of the bedroom awoke in her a hunger so sharp and intense she found it difficult to breathe. "Wh-where are you going?"

"Topside. We dock in two hours."

"A dawn piano recital?"

He slipped into his shirt. "I do more than play piano."

"A regular jack-of-all-trades," she observed sleepily.

"You do what you have to do." He reached for his shirt. "You have a problem with that?"

"No," she answered, meeting his eyes. "I admire it."

He sat down on the edge of the bed to put on his shoes. "I didn't think you admired much of anything about me, Meggie."

She touched his arm. "What's wrong? Last night was so—"

"Last night was last night," he said, standing up again. "We'd both be smart to keep things in perspective."

"My perspective is fine," she snapped. "We were looking for great sex and we found it. Case closed."

"You know," he said, "I was wrong. You haven't changed. You're still the same sharp-tongued—"

She threw her pillow at him. "Shut up! I don't care what you think of me. Your opinion doesn't matter."

She was naked. Angry. Wild-eyed.

*Naked.*

He stopped in the doorway, blood heating in his veins.

"Jake...." Part warning, part invitation.

"Shut up," he said, striding toward her. "Don't say anything."

She was in his arms in a heartbeat. Passionate.

Warm. Demanding. She knew what he wanted before he did. He backed her up against the wall. Her hands found the zipper on his fly. She wrapped her legs around his hips and he plunged into her aching body with an urgency that bordered on brutal. She loved every second of it.

Their lovemaking was fierce. It wasn't about tenderness. It wasn't about desire.

It was about something that shouldn't be happening, something they were powerless to stop. It was about the girl she'd been and the man he was and all the failed dreams that would haunt them for the rest of their lives.

"What are we going to do?" she asked as he dressed for the second time that morning. "This is—"

"Incredible," he said, zipping his pants.

"And out of control."

"That's the point, Megan. We have two more days to let it run its course before we're back in Miami."

"What if it hasn't run its course?" The words were out before she could stop them.

"It will have. We're wrong for each other, Meggie. Always have been. Always will be."

"I know," she whispered. "I know."

She wondered what he would say if he knew they had a child. A beautiful little girl with his eyes and his laugh and his passion for life.

They might be wrong for each other, but they had done something terribly right when they'd created Jenny.

"...meet me this afternoon in front of La Playa Real."

She blinked. "What?"

"This afternoon," he repeated. "We don't sail until eight o'clock."

"I thought you had a meeting." Ostensibly that was why he'd made his dramatic entrance through the secret panel in the hallway.

"I do, but I'll bail out early."

"I don't want you to lose your job, Jake." She wasn't being altruistic. She simply didn't want it on her conscience.

"Don't worry about my job." He bent down and kissed her thoroughly. "The clock's ticking, Megan. Let's make the most of it."

MEGAN SWORE SHE WASN'T going to meet him. God knew, she had every reason not to. What had happened between them was beyond explanation. Six long years had vanished at the first intoxicating feel of skin against skin and Megan had responded like one possessed, but that was no reason to think it had to happen a second time.

She didn't want to feel this way. She'd wanted to discover his magic had disappeared along with their marriage, that she could live without magic and warm kisses and dreams she no longer believed could come true.

But La Mirada was far from reality. The island was a verdant swell of land southwest of Nassau, one of those lushly beautiful places that seemed designed strictly to put people in the mood for romance.

Bougainvillea bloomed everywhere you looked. Beach roses vied with gardenias for room. The houses were pastel confections of lemon and mint and sky blue with wrought-iron grillwork and window boxes overflowing with geraniums. It was easy to forget there was a real world out there.

Back home she might be able to convince herself she was happy with the status quo, but there in that lush Caribbean paradise it was hard to imagine being satisfied with anything less than the splendor she'd found last night in his arms.

"I wish you were coming with us," Val said as she and Megan parted company in town. "Tropicale is flying us over to Freeport to visit the casinos."

"Sounds terrific," Megan answered, "but I thought I'd do a little sight-seeing right here."

Val shrugged. "To each her own. See you at dinner, Megan." She hurried off to catch up with her sister and the rest of the group who were boarding the jitney bus that would take them to the tiny airport.

Megan watched as the bus rattled down the street. It disappeared around the corner, leaving her alone.

But not really.

She sensed his presence as strongly as she had the first night aboard ship. A bone-deep awareness of the swell of her breasts, the curve of her hips, the way she held her head. The awareness was almost painful.

"You're late," he complained, stepping out from the shadows.

"Not very."

"Having second thoughts?"

"No," she said as he approached, all male swagger and splendor. His jeans were faded. His smile was bright. "Are you?"

He took her arm, the pressure of his fingers blatantly possessive. ''Ask me again in a few hours.''

Suddenly the thought of spending more than a few minutes alone with her ex-husband seemed an exercise in insanity. Forty-eight hours ago Jake had been nothing more than a memory, a part of Megan's past that she could summon up at will or relegate to the farthest corner of her mind. But there was no way she could dismiss the man next to her. He commanded attention. She saw it in the glances of the women strolling past, in the way other men moved aside to make way for him as they started down the narrow cobblestone street.

In her own acquiescence to the force of his will.

A ripple of anticipation ran up her spine. *This is why you're here,* she reminded herself as Jake led her up a narrow path that wound its way up a steep hill lined with bougainvillea and gardenias. She wanted the passion between them to blaze hotter than the sun overhead, then burn itself out once and for all.

They picked their way over the uneven road toward El Cielo, a sixteenth-century fort on the eastern side of the tiny island. Jake seemed to know the island by heart, from the twisting roads to the history of the fort.

''How did you learn so much about La Mirada?'' she asked.

''I lived here for a few months after we divorced.''

''A bit off the beaten path, isn't it?''

''That's what I was looking for.''

''I remember,'' she murmured. *Don't ask me to be like your father, Meggie...there's more to life than the bottom line and stock options when you retire....* She cleared her throat. "Still planning to sail around the world?"

"Someday," he replied, meeting her eyes. "When I find the right person to sail with me."

His meaning was unmistakable. For once she didn't avoid it. "I was never part of your dream."

"You could have been."

She said nothing. There were other dreams, as well, dreams he knew nothing about. *We have a daughter, Jake…a little girl with your eyes and your laugh and the same reckless love of life….* She cast about for a more neutral topic. "Where did you live?"

"A beach house on the other side of the bay. Moody electricity, no hot water." His grin was bemused. "But a great view of the ocean."

They made their way up a narrow, hilly street that wound along the edge of a cliff. Megan felt like she was strolling down a charming side street in Madrid or Barcelona. The curlicued trims and cornices of the tiny stucco bungalows were painted a dazzling white and gleamed in the sun. Fire-engine red geraniums overflowed the window boxes, a vivid touch of color against the pale facades.

She didn't have to try very hard to imagine him living in one of those bungalows, spending his days on the sandy beach and his nights in the arms of a woman who asked for no more than he was willing to give. He'd never lived by the rules. Nine-to-five and three-piece suits were as foreign to Jake as astral projection.

Her father had been only too happy to point out the benefits to be gained by marrying the daughter of one of the richest businessmen in Florida. "Jake isn't one for the long haul," Darrin McLean had said. "If you were the daughter of a plumber, don't think he would've swept you off to Las Vegas the way he did. He's an Aussie, princess. His great-grandfather was probably a convict with a record a mile long. You can't trust a man like that."

What a joke that was. When all was said and done, it was her father who'd thrown her to the wolves.

She brushed aside the memory. What difference did it make anyway? She and Jake were divorced. They would remain divorced. With a little luck, once this weekend was over, the last hold he had over her would finally be broken and she could take the first step toward finding a man who would love her and need her and cherish her—all of the things Jake could never do.

Men like Jake were meant to be enjoyed, then chalked up to one of life's more interesting experiences.

She hadn't understood that at nineteen.

Now she did and it made all the difference.

Ten minutes later they reached a daunting set of stone steps.

She peered up the staircase. "I don't suppose there's an elevator hidden away someplace."

"No escalators either. Got the stamina?"

"We'll find out." She straightened her shoulders and took a deep breath. "Lead the way, Lockwood."

The twentieth century dropped away from them as they climbed the stairs, taking them back in time to the age of Columbus and the dawn of colonization in the New World.

"My God," she breathed as they entered the stone fortress. "I had no idea...."

"Incredible, isn't it?"

The grayish brown stone walls were rough to the touch, slightly damp against the palm of her hand. Bricks, faded with time, outlined the doors and windows. "It's so cool in here," she murmured. "So peaceful." *So private*.

There were no guardrails at the uppermost point and Megan held her breath as Jake stood on the narrow ledge, arms folded across his chest, head thrown back against the wind, as if defying some ancient god to accept his challenge. One hundred forty feet below them, the waves pounded against the walls of the fortress, a reminder of the awesome power of nature unleashed.

"You haven't changed at all," she whispered into the wind. Still wild and reckless and filled with more passion for life than any ten people she'd ever known. He didn't give a damn about the future. He lived for the moment, collecting sensations the way other people collected stamps.

The wind whistled around the curves of the tower, whipping her hair against her cheeks in a tangle that matched her emotions. She rummaged in her bag for a clip or rubber band, grateful for the diversion.

Jake sat down next to her on the narrow battlement. "What's wrong? I thought you were enjoying the view."

That was putting it mildly. "Too much hair," she said instead, gathering the silky mass into a ponytail and holding it back with one hand. "One day I'm going to go out and get a buzz cut."

"Let me."

Before she could protest, he leaned over and, placing his hands on either temple, pinned her auburn hair back with his long fingers. His index fingers rested on the tiny pulse that beat on either side of her forehead.

The look in his eyes was dark, compelling. She wanted to look away, to prove to him that his power over her was only as strong as she allowed it to be, but even she knew the folly of that idea.

There was no place to hide.

HER PULSE POUNDED beneath his fingertips. He cradled her head in his hands. She raised her smoky green eyes to meet his. He recognized the invitation.

"Megan?"

She nodded.

He moved closer.

She tilted her head.

He bent low.

Her lips parted.

He—

"'Scuse me, but y'all look to be Americans, right?"

The intruder wore a plaid cotton shirt, cutoffs, and sandals. A big black camera, complete with zoom lens, dangled from a strap slung around his neck. The fact that he didn't kill the poor guy was a testament to Jake's self-control.

"Say, I don't mean to butt in, but my wife and I got ourselves a bit of a problem." The man pointed toward a tiny blond woman in a demure pink outfit who stood by the guardhouse. "You *are* Americans, right?"

"One of us," Jake said with little grace. "I'm from Oz."

"Australia," Megan explained, noticing their puzzlement.

The groom smiled. "Sue and me are on our honeymoon and we'd appreciate it if you'd snap a picture of us over there. We'd be much obliged."

Jake looked to Megan who nodded.

"You got it," said Jake with reluctant grace.

The guy handed the camera to Jake. "It's all set." He positioned himself next to his blushing bride. "All you gotta do is push the button."

The pair broke into enormous grins and Jake snapped three quick shots. They were so happy it hurt to look at them. Megan tried to remember if she'd ever been that happy in her entire life.

*Last night,* a voice whispered. *Last night in his arms....*

There was something terribly innocent about new love, a certain fragile beauty that rarely withstood the onslaught of the outside world. Most couples managed to find something deeper, a love more resilient to the ravages of time. Sometimes she wondered if, given time, she and Jake might have managed a miracle of their own.

"Ma'am?"

She glanced up to find the young bride smiling at her. "If you give us your camera, we'll take pictures of you and your husband."

"Good idea," her groom enthused. "What's a honeymoon without snapshots?"

The right words just wouldn't come to her. How did you tell a starry-eyed young couple with rice in their hair that this man was your ex-husband and the only thing you had in common with him was a physical compatibility that defied logic. They'd find out soon enough that marriage wasn't all moonlight and roses.

To her amazement, Jake seemed to understand. "Come on," he coaxed. "One picture for posterity."

He sat next to her on the ledge and put his arm around her shoulders.

"Smile pretty," he drawled. "It'll make the kids happy."

Sitting in the brilliant sunshine in the ageless serenity of El Cielo, she had no trouble smiling pretty for the kids.

"Now you just give me your address," said the bride to Megan, "and I'll make sure to send you two a copy the minute Kevin and I get home."

Megan scribbled her work address on a slip of paper.

"That's just the most adorable little pendant," the bride cooed, gesturing toward the four-leaf clover. "Where did you get it?"

Megan froze for an instant. "A good friend," she replied, as Jenny seemed to materialize between her and Jake.

The bride smiled and pocketed Megan's address. "Now you can count on these pictures."

"Be happy," Megan breathed, impulsively hugging

the surprised young woman. "Take good care of each other."

The newlyweds left and once more Megan and Jake were alone.

Jake fingered the four-leaf clover pendant. "Since when do you travel without diamonds?"

Megan shrugged, feeling the pull of home. "No one travels with their good jewelry these days, Jake."

"That little bride had her good jewelry on." He laughed, but there was no malice in it. "Her diamond was even smaller than the one I gave you."

"They're so young," Megan said softly. "I don't think we were ever that young."

"You were."

She shook her head. "Not like that."

"You were wide-eyed and innocent. I'd never seen anyone like you before."

She lifted her chin. "You don't stay innocent long in Palm Beach, Jake."

"You did."

Her body heated at the memory. "It seems so long ago."

She tried to remember how it had felt to be young and hopeful but that particular memory eluded her. To her amazement Jake seemed to sense her mood.

"Come with me." He reached for her hand, then led her across the slippery, mossy bricks to the *garito,* one of the guardhouses that overlooked the surrounding moat. She smelled salt and dampness and she could easily imagine the hundreds of Spanish guards who had stood in this same spot, watching the sea for signs of the invading British or Dutch navies.

She also was painfully aware of Jake's warmth. They were both silent, listening to the Atlantic crashing against the rocks below. She placed her bare elbows on the rough brick ledge and rested her chin in her hands. She inhaled deeply of the clean ocean air and the intoxicating scent of Jake's skin, slightly musky and very male. A vibrating current of electricity was humming through her body.

He took his time. She shivered as he drew his hands up her bare arms, across her tanned shoulders, then up her throat and to her mouth. He drew one finger across her moist, slightly open lips and, on impulse, she caught it between her strong white teeth and bit lightly down on the flesh.

He laughed and leaned forward, his hard mouth slanting down across hers. His lips demanded a response and she met his demands. He held her gently by the hips while she wrapped her arms around his neck and allowed herself the exquisite luxury of plunging her fingers into his thick hair.

She gasped as his tongue entered her willing mouth. Eager...demanding. He drew responses from her that she never knew she was capable of. Palms flat, he traced the curve of her hips, in to her waist and up and around her full breasts that strained against the thin cotton of her sundress. She trembled under his touch and was aware of her nipples hardening against the feel of his palms.

He whispered something against her throat in a voice so soft she wondered if she had imagined it.

Her eyes fluttered open as he burned kisses along the curve of her breasts. He put a hand on either side of her face, thumbs pressing lightly against her cheek-bones.

"Alone at last." His words were dark with promise.

"They were sweet," Megan countered. "I—"

He kissed her quiet, his body moving against hers in a way that made her blood run hot. His hand slid down her side, easing her skirt up.

She thought she would die from anticipation. It had been so long since she'd felt like this, so long since she'd felt like a woman that she was helpless against the desire building inside her. "Jake," she managed. "We can't..." She gasped as his fingers slid inside the leg of her lacy panties. "There's no room to— someone might see us."

"I don't give a damn if someone sees us," he said.

He'd always found danger exciting. Once they'd made love in the back row of an empty movie theater, Megan astride him, until they came together in a shuddering and silent climax that left them hungry for more.

He grasped her by the hips, his fingers pressing into the curve of her buttocks. "Wrap your legs around me and I'll—"

She glanced about, both nervous and excited. "Do you see anyone?"

"There's no one here, Meggie. No one but us."

He found her moist center with his fingertips, separating her, caressing her, stroking her deeper and deeper, until she came in a long, shuddering wave of sensation.

He held her against him as she rode out the storm. She couldn't have felt more exposed if she'd stood there naked in the tropical sunlight. But it didn't matter. He'd stripped her bare even though she hadn't removed an item of clothing, tearing away her defenses until she found herself powerless before her need.

"Mommy! Somebody's *in* there!" A high-pitched voice at the opening to the *garito* made them jump. A small red-haired girl with curious blue eyes peered in at them.

Megan stifled a small shriek and pulled away from Jake, pushing her skirt back into place.

An older woman grabbed the child by the wrist. She glanced quickly from Jake to Megan, then blushed furiously. "Amy, come over here and leave the people alone."

"But, Mommy—"

"Amy, *now!* They're on their honeymoon and they want to be alone."

The spell was broken.

"That's the second time," he muttered as they went down the worn stairs to the ground level. "What the hell's going on?"

"Pheromones. They're in the air. Can you imagine how the newlyweds would feel if they knew we were divorced?"

"I guess we can let them have their illusions," he said as they crossed the wide expanse of manicured grass that led back to the road.

She understood all about illusions. Happily ever after was an illusion.

But those kisses in the *garito,* the electricity that had flowed between them—

No.

They had been very real.

And if she wasn't careful those kisses would be her undoing.

## Chapter Six

"This isn't going to work," Jake announced as they reached the main street. "Half the damn island was in there."

Megan looked at him, eyes wide and curious. A touch uncertain. He still hadn't grown accustomed to that look of vulnerability. It made her more accessible, less the arrogant girl he'd first loved. It made her more of a woman...and a hell of a lot more dangerous than he'd ever imagined.

Suddenly the whole thing seemed crazy. Those interruptions back in the *garito* had been masterfully timed, pulling him back to reality. Jake had never had difficulty separating sex from emotions, but last night with Megan he'd found it impossible. He'd known the sex would be explosive, but this deeper sense of connection between them was something he hadn't expected or wanted.

She was supposed to be the bitch goddess he'd married. The Palm Beach deb who dabbled in catering while someone back home did all the hard work.

She wasn't supposed to be a flesh-and-blood woman

with insecurities and a look of sadness that made him long to tell her he'd take care of her.

*So tell her the truth, Lockwood. Tell her you own the* Sea Goddess *and* Tropicale *and houses that put her father's Palm Beach palace to shame.*

This was the moment he'd been working toward since the day she'd left him and slipped back into the life she'd known and loved long before he'd come onto the scene.

But where in hell was the sense of exhilaration, the sheer burst of satisfaction he'd figured would be part of the mix?

Abruptly he wheeled to the left and propelled her along a cobbled pathway that wound its way through the alley that bisected the shopping district. The damp stones were covered with moss and the smells of earth and heat rose up from the ground and surrounded them.

"Where are we going?" Megan asked as they exited the alleyway and started up a steep hill.

"Someplace where we won't be interrupted."

"Jake, I—"

He pulled her into his arms, then claimed her mouth with his. She was hot and sweet and he wanted to take her right there in the blazing sun, lay her down on the damp grass and bury himself inside her body. He told her exactly that and she swayed toward him, moth to a flame.

"There's a small marina over the hill where we can rent a rowboat," he rasped when he was able to form a coherent sentence again.

She nodded, her beautiful face flushed with desire

that matched his. She'd never learned the fine art of dissembling—not about sex. From the very beginning she'd accepted the sensual side of her nature with enthusiasm and his fists clenched involuntarily at the thought of another man learning the sweet secrets of her body. The secrets he'd unlocked for her a long time ago.

They crested the hill and, as if on cue, the marina appeared below them, a small perfect jewel set against the sapphire brilliance of the ocean. Two small schooners waited proudly in the tranquil waters. A nest of rowboats, their deep green color faded from the unrelenting tropical sunshine, bobbed impatiently, tugging at the ropes that held them fast to the end of the dock.

"Wait here," he ordered. "I'll get us a boat."

MEGAN STOOD TO ONE SIDE of the narrow dock as Jake, speaking in a fluid ribbon of Spanish, charmed the young girl in charge into renting one of the disreputable-looking rowboats.

Minutes later he helped her into a boat and, manning the oars, guided the vessel out onto the lake. She watched as the muscles of his chest and shoulders flexed with each stroke. He rowed the way he did everything else, with power and assurance, and they quickly left the marina behind.

The air was sultry, heady with the scent of exotic flowers and expectations. It occurred to her that this was dangerous, that nothing good could come from living your fantasies, but the thought vanished as quickly as it had come. This was exactly what she needed, to immerse herself in dreams, to give herself up to sensation without regard for the world she'd left behind when she boarded the *Sea Goddess* a few short days ago.

His voice broke into her thoughts. "Over there," he indicated. "The other side of the cove."

She saw a tiny whitewashed stucco house, surrounded by a wild mass of exotic flowers and greenery that led down to the shore. It had an air of rakish charm, not unlike the charm of the man who'd once been her husband. Curious, she glanced back at Jake.

"That's where I lived after the divorce," he said.

"Alone?" The words were in the air before she could stop them.

He met her eyes. "Some of the time."

She hated herself for the stab of jealousy his answer evoked. "What made you leave? This island is paradise." Exactly the type of hedonistic wonderland he would have loved.

"Even paradise gets boring after a while."

She should have known better than to ask. There was nothing of forever about Jake Lockwood and there never had been. Still it pleased her to know he hadn't found his elusive happy ending here in the arms of another woman.

He crossed the oars and leaned forward. "Feel like seeing how the other half lives?"

She bristled. "What's that supposed to mean?"

"Claws in, Meggie." He gestured toward the bungalow. "I'm talking about a guided tour."

"You still rent it?"

"Let's just say I have access."

"Spare me the explanation, please." She didn't want to hear about some wealthy older woman with a seven-figure bank account and a penchant for sexy piano players.

"I wasn't about to give you one."

She had a biting retort at the ready when a sound like rushing water caught her attention. "How seaworthy is this thing?"

He glanced down at a small leak near his right foot. "That's nothing to worry about."

She gestured toward the mini-geyser behind him. "How about that one?"

He looked over his shoulder. "Minor annoyance."

"That minor annoyance is getting bigger, Jake. You'd better start bailing water."

His scowl was something to behold. "We don't need to bail water," he snapped. "We're fine." She did notice, however, that he was rowing again with renewed vigor.

"The water's up to my ankles." Megan pointed toward her wet feet in her strappy red sandals. "We're not going to make it to shore."

"We'll make it," he snarled through clenched teeth.

"We must be two hundred yards away," she persisted. "The only way we're going to make it is if we swim."

He looked as if he'd like to toss her overboard. "We're not swimming. We'll get there in this boat."

"I don't think so." The water was approaching her calves. "The only way this boat is going to make it is if we tow it ashore."

"Maybe if you'd quit complaining and start bailing water we'd be in better shape."

"You know what?" said Megan, rising to her feet. "I think I'd rather bail out than bail water." And with that she dived into the water and headed toward land.

The water was warm, delightfully silky against her skin. She couldn't remember the last time she'd done anything so spontaneous, so crazy, and the sensation of freedom was intoxicating.

"Come on in, Jake," she called as she floated lazily on her back. "The captain doesn't have to go down with his ship."

He ignored her and kept on rowing.

She laughed, the sound bouncing off the water. "Oh, the stubborn male ego," she chided, swimming toward him. "You never were good at admitting you were wrong."

"I'm not wrong." His words were clipped. Megan couldn't suppress a grin. "There's nothing wrong with this damn rowboat."

"Right," said Megan as she swam parallel. "You'll just ignore the fact that you're sinking faster than the *Titanic*."

He grunted something rude and kept on rowing. "I'll reach land before you will."

She glided along next to him. "I don't think so."

"Bet me."

"I'd hate to take your hard-earned money."

"Shut up," he growled as the rowboat listed to starboard.

"Getting hot under the collar, Lockwood?" She

grabbed hold of the side of the boat and grinned up at him. "I think you need to cool off."

"Do it and you're a dead woman."

She arched her brows. "Is that a dare, mighty Mr. Lockwood?"

"Don't push it, Megan," he warned.

"I think it's a dare," she said, "and you know how I feel about dares."

"Try it and I'll—"

Megan was pleasantly surprised to find how easy it was to overturn a rowboat with an ex-husband in it. He even made quite a satisfying splash when he hit the water. The fact that he was going to be mad as hell when he surfaced didn't even dampen her enthusiasm. Treading water, she waited for him to appear. And waited. And waited some more.

"This isn't funny, Jake," she said, glancing around.

No response.

"I'm not laughing."

Still nothing.

"You can swim," she murmured, dog-paddling around the perimeter of the rapidly sinking rowboat. "I know you can swim." She stopped, treading water. "Can't you?"

A terrible thought struck her. Had she ever seen him swim even once during their marriage? God knew she'd enjoyed the sight of him in his swim trunks but for the life of her she couldn't remember ever seeing those trunks put to use.

She took a deep breath, then dived beneath the surface. The salt water stung her eyes and she could barely see a foot ahead of her. Her heart thundered painfully inside her chest as she kicked hard, propelling herself toward bottom.

Two minutes later, her lungs bursting, Megan rose to the surface.

"Took you long enough," said a familiar voice.

Gasping for air, she turned in the direction of the sound. "Jake?"

"Who else?"

"I thought something terrible had happened to you."

"You should've thought of that before you sank the damn boat."

He struck out from the boat, his muscular arms cutting through the water with frightening efficiency.

"You louse," she muttered. "You swim like a damn fish."

His laughter floated back toward her, deep and full and unbearably male. She was a strong swimmer but no match for him. He reached shore before she did, then waited for her, jeans plastered to his legs, his shirt molded to his powerful torso in a way that was quite remarkable.

Her knees scraped the sand and she scrambled to her feet. Her red and white cotton sundress had seemed a perfectly demure choice when she'd plucked it from her closet this morning. Unfortunately she hadn't taken an impromptu swim into account. She had only to look at Jake, with his magnificent body backlit by the sun, to know how revealing her outfit must be. Feeling awkward and more than a little self-conscious, she fought the urge to dive back into the water and swim for the safety of the open seas.

SHE WAS SELF-CONSCIOUS. Who would've believed it? Beautiful, arrogant Megan McLean who had spent her entire life basking in the glow of approval from everyone she met. He could see it in the way she ducked her head as she made her way from the water, in the slope of her shoulders and sway of her hips. She wasn't daring him to look at her, the way she would have years ago. Instead she seemed as if she'd rather he didn't look at her at all. Was it possible she'd forgotten how incredible she was?

Her breasts were clearly visible through the wet cotton bodice of her dress. Her nipples pushed against the fabric, hard and asking to be sucked. Her skirt hugged her belly and hips, the heavy folds outlining her thighs, hinting at what lay hidden between them. She looked lush, juicy, tempting as hell. And so vulnerable it damn near broke his heart.

To his surprise he found he didn't just want her, he wanted to know what had brought about the change. He wondered what had happened in the six years since their divorce to soften the sharp edges of her personality, to make her less an ice princess and more a flesh-and-blood woman. He knew it shouldn't matter. The facts of her life were none of his business. Who she'd slept with, who'd made her laugh or cry.

He wondered what she'd say if he asked her to throw caution to the winds and sail off with him. The idea had a certain appeal. There was nothing tying her down. At least nothing she'd mentioned. Her partner could take care of the business. Knowing Megan, her involvement was more window-dressing than anything else.

He'd learned a lot about the rich since the days of their marriage. People who were born to luxuries like yachts and limousines and trust funds didn't look at the world the same way as people who had to work for those luxuries. When they went to work it was more to be in step with nineties sensibilities than it was to earn a living.

Megan was who she was. That wasn't going to change. He understood that. And now he could finally afford her.

Tonight, he thought. Tonight he'd tell her about the Tropicale, about what he'd done with his past and his plans for the future. He'd tell her that what had started out as a way to settle old scores had turned into something even more dangerous.

But as she walked toward him something gripped him, a sensation so strong, so overpowering that he wanted to turn back the clock and try to make things right....

*THEY HAD DRIVEN UP from Miami to retrieve the last of her things from the pink palace where she'd lived with her father. Jake had been braced for another fight, but McLean was out of town on business and he had found himself almost disappointed.*

*"It's better this way," Megan had said as she tossed silk blouses and gold necklaces into a leather suitcase. "Daddy just needs time to get used to the idea that I'm married." She turned to him, a smile on her beautiful lips. "He's really a wonderful man, Jake. I know you two will be friends." Her smile widened. "Daddy wants to help us...he even said he'd buy us*

*a little house in the neighborhood so we can all be
together.''*

*Something inside Jake snapped. ''You're not
Daddy's little girl anymore,'' he'd said, turning the
suitcase upside down on the bed. ''You're my wife.''*

*''Jake!'' She'd sounded surprised. A touch fearful.
''What on earth—''*

*''Leave it,'' he ordered, scattering the expensive
clothes across the floor. ''You don't need any of it.''*

*She scrambled around, gathering up silk blouses
and snakeskin shoes. ''These are my things. I'm not
going anywhere without them.''*

*''The hell you're not.''*

*''These clothes belong to me.''*

*''They belong to your old man.''*

*''They're mine.''*

*''You don't get it,'' he said in amazement. He
wanted to wring her lovely neck. ''I'll buy you new
clothes.''*

*The look on her face spoke volumes. There was a
hell of a big difference between K mart dresses and
Donna Karan originals. Even he knew that.*

*''Isn't that foolish, Jake, when I already have so
many wonderful things?''*

*His gaze traveled the room. The furniture probably
cost more than he'd made in his life. Heavy damask
drapes. Antique dressing table. Cozy family pictures
in silver frames. He thought of the station in Western
Queensland where he'd grown up, of the pallet where
he'd slept in the kitchen because there wasn't a room
for him in the tiny house.*

*Who the hell was he to tell her to leave her belong-*

*ings behind when he couldn't afford to buy her even
one of those fancy outfits that filled her closet? Mc-
Lean had told Jake what he thought of their chances.
The bastard's words ate at his gut like a cancer. Six
months at the most...you can't expect a girl like Megan to live hand-to-mouth....*

*McLean didn't think Jake knew what poverty could
do to a woman, but he did. He'd watched his sister,
Angie, die a little every day as she cooked and cleaned
and dreamed away her life in that shack they'd called
home. Only forty years old, she was destined to spend
the rest of her days caring for their father and tending
the land, while her beauty faded like the homespun
curtains at their kitchen window.*

*"Why are you looking at me like that, Jake?" Me-
gan's feathery brows were knotted in a frown.*

*"Come here." His voice was rough. His emotions
were running high.*

*She knew what he was about. "Not here!" Her
laugh was nervous and delighted both, as he crossed
the room to where she stood. "Someone might see
us."*

*He kicked shut the door. "Nobody will see us."*

*She giggled as he pulled her into his arms. "I can't
do it in my old room, Jake. It's—"*

*"Exciting." He cupped her breasts. "The word
you're looking for is 'exciting.'"*

*She moaned as he moved against her. "What if
Daddy comes home?"*

*"Shut up," he commanded, claiming her mouth. He
didn't want to hear about Daddy or the servants,
about fancy clothes and privileged lives. He wanted to*

*claim her in the oldest way possible. The most prim-
itive. And he took her, fast and hot and hard, in the
room where she'd grown up, surrounded by all the
things he'd never be able to provide for her. Not in a
million years.*

*When she cried out his name, a high fierce cry of
ecstasy, he'd almost believed they could make it work.*

WE SHOULD'VE TALKED *to each other,* he thought as she
made her way toward him with the grace that was as
much a part of her as her auburn hair and sharp intel-
lect. Making love had been easy. Maybe too easy. Perfectly mated physically they'd paid no attention to the
other puzzle pieces that made up the whole of a marriage.

"Jake." Megan stopped a few feet from him. Her
green eyes were wide and questioning. "Why are you
looking at me like that?"

"Because you're beautiful," he stated, unable to
stop the words. "And because I was wondering how
life would have been if you weren't."

"We never would have married, for starters."

The cynicism in her voice took him by surprise and
he said so.

"I don't know why you're surprised," she replied.
"Sexual chemistry is what our marriage was all about,
wasn't it? I think I was in some kind of erotic haze
from the moment we met until the moment—" She
stopped abruptly and looked away.

He finished it for her. "Until the moment you
walked out."

"That about says it all." She met his eyes once

again. "We were never very good at conversation, were we?"

"No, Meggie," he admitted. "Not very good at all."

They'd used sex to get closer...and to stay farther apart. Substituting sex for intimacy had been so easy, so natural, that it had never occurred to either one of them that there was more to marriage than what happened between the sheets.

"You know, you're a lot...nicer than I remembered."

He grinned. "And you're a lot more perceptive."

She tilted her head to one side. "Do you hear that?"

He listened. "Birds singing?"

"Conversation, Lockwood. We're having a real live conversation. Can you believe it?"

"Too bad we didn't think of it six years ago."

"Yes," Megan whispered, her eyes glistening. "Too bad." She shivered despite the hot sun and wrapped her arms across her chest. *There is so much I need to say to you, Jake, and I don't know how to begin....*

"Come on," he urged. "We'd better get these clothes dry before we head back to the yacht."

She gripped his forearm. "The ship! How on earth will we get back there, Jake? What if they sail without us?"

"They won't sail without us."

"How can you be so sure?"

He flashed the piratical grin that had first won her heart. "They need me, Meggie. Can't have a cruise without a piano player. International law." *You blew it again, Lockwood. You had the perfect chance to tell her the truth and you were too damn yellow to take advantage of it.*

He took her hand and led her toward the cottage. "There's a laundry room off the kitchen," he said as he unlocked the door. "We'll toss these things in the dryer. While they're drying I'll make a few calls and see if I can scare us up another rowboat."

He ushered Megan into the cool, dimly lit front room. She glanced about, taking note of the pale stucco walls, the spare furniture, the total absence of sound. "What makes you think the phone is hooked up?"

"Positive thinking." He lifted the receiver of the wall unit in the kitchen. "See?" He punched in a few numbers. "It's working."

She arched a brow in his general direction but said nothing. The past few days had been one unbelievable turn of events after another. It wouldn't surprise her if the leaky rowboat appeared on the shore, all repaired and ready to go.

The kitchen was stripped to the bare essentials. Tiny refrigerator. Tiny stove. A small porcelain sink with a window that looked out over the scruffy backyard. Bracing her elbows on the sill, she gazed through the dusty glass and tried to imagine Jake living in this place.

So this was where he'd been when her father died, when she was alone and pregnant and so deeply in debt she couldn't pay her doctor's bills. He'd been living in a tumbledown cottage on some godforsaken island in the middle of nowhere. She didn't know whether to laugh or cry.

*I know how it feels now, Jake. I know all about living hand-to-mouth, about worrying how I'm going to pay the bills, about things like need and ambition and being responsible for someone who's too young and too immature to be responsible for herself.*

She chuckled softly. Only difference was Jenny was five years old while Megan had been nineteen.

Once again Jake was speaking Spanish. She caught the words "rowboat" and "trouble," but he spoke so rapidly that her high school Spanish couldn't keep pace. Moving to the laundry room, she wrinkled her nose at the age of the big washer and dryer but beggars couldn't be choosers.

If she went back to the *Sea Goddess* looking like something caught in a fisherman's net, she could kiss her contract with Tropicale goodbye. She'd had more than her fill of being the object of the gossip mongers when her father died. She wasn't about to go through that again.

Quickly she stripped off her sundress and tossed it into the dryer. She hesitated for a moment over her panties but then decided the time was long past for false modesty and they joined the sundress.

"I made a few calls and I can get us a rowboat from a guy a mile up the road," Jake called, his footsteps growing louder as he approached the laundry room. "You stay here and I'll—"

He stopped in the doorway, mesmerized by the sight of her naked. It wasn't like he hadn't seen her that way before. He had. Many times and in many places.

And each time he'd experienced the same flare of desire in the center of his gut. This time, however, it was different. The desire was there but it was tempered with a feeling so intense, so unexpected, that he found himself struggling for composure.

Maybe he was crazy but for a second he seemed to see beyond her beauty, beyond their past, straight inside her vulnerable and lonely heart.

"There are some T-shirts in the bedroom," he mumbled, turning away.

"Your clothes," she said. "Let me dry them."

"The sun can do that." He started for the door. "I'll be back in a few minutes."

He was gone before she could say another word.

IT DIDN'T TAKE LONG for Megan's sundress to dry. She slipped it back on, wincing at the wrinkled skirt, then managed to arrange her mane of hair into a fairly presentable French braid. She wandered through the cottage, poking her head into closets and cupboards while she tried to imagine how it had been when Jake lived there.

Actually the cottage wasn't much smaller than the house she and Jenny lived in now. Strange to think there'd been a time when she would have turned up her nose at anything less than five thousand square feet. She could have been happy here, living with Jake, working toward the future. Too bad she hadn't realized it six years ago when they'd still had a chance.

She stepped outside, then followed the path down to the beach. The air was warm, heavy with the scent of flowers and the sharp, salty tang of the sea. A stab of longing pierced her heart as she thought of Jenny. *Oh, sweetheart, what am I doing to you?* It had all seemed so clear, so logical, before today.

She sat by the water's edge, arms wrapped about her knees, her thoughts tangled. Jenny wanted a father desperately. And no one knew better than Megan how important a father's love could be. Jake wasn't the same man he'd been during their marriage. The man she'd married wouldn't have been caught dead playing piano on some other man's yacht. He would have been off tilting at windmills, dreaming crazy dreams that could never come true.

And those dreams hadn't come true. Not a one of them. He wasn't rich or famous or powerful. He wasn't any of the things he'd wanted to be back when they were married and yet he acted as if everything he had ever wanted was his for the taking. He had changed. No doubt about it.

But had he changed enough to be the kind of father Jenny deserved or would he someday break their little girl's heart the way Darrin McLean had broken hers? Jenny deserved a hero but Megan knew heroes were as elusive as happy endings.

FRANÇOIS AND HIS WIFE, Claudine, were the kind of neighbors who wouldn't take no for an answer. All Jake wanted was their rowboat. He ended up with the rowboat, a bottle of champagne, a bag of plums, and a half-dozen white orchids.

And François and Claudine.

"You don't have to do this," he told them as they

loaded everything into their Land Rover. "I'll row myself back."

"Nonsense," said François, his accent a blend of French, Spanish and boarding school English. "It has been too long since we saw you."

"And aeons since we've seen you with a young lady." Claudine dimpled, her lined face still lovely despite the years. "La Mirada is a quiet port of call, Jake. Surely you know we feast on the romances of others."

Claudine and François caught him up on local gossip as the Land Rover bumped over the dirt road that led to his cottage. Jake heard only part of it. He was too busy berating himself for letting these two incurable romantics know that he had a woman with him.

Still he had to admit there was something infectious about their enthusiasm and zest for life that reminded him of all the things he'd liked about living on La Mirada. Warm company. Great food. The Disneyland beauty of the island. All the good things in life that he wanted to recover when he set sail on his boat. He was ambitious enough to enjoy the day-to-day combat of business, but a part of him was still a kid from Queensland, longing to see the world.

François angled his vehicle onto the sandy strip that passed for a driveway, then turned off the ignition. "The parking brake," Claudine reminded him.

François grumbled but he complied. "Old woman, mind your own business."

"You are my business," Claudine said. "No one else would have you."

The affection between the husband and wife was

obvious in every word and gesture that passed between them. Jake found himself wondering how it would have been for him and Megan if they'd managed to make a go of their own marriage but he couldn't bring the picture to life. The sex he could imagine in vivid detail. But the ordinary give-and-take that made up the fabric of a marriage was as alien to him as the concept of happily ever after.

He helped François unfasten the rowboat from the trailer hitched to the rear of the Land Rover. He intended to drag the boat down to the water but François insisted on holding up his end of the endeavor. Claudine gathered together the wine and fruit and cheese and followed behind.

"Maybe you'd better wait here," Jake said as he slid the rowboat into the water. It had occurred to him that Megan might be stark naked and not in the mood for greeting unexpected visitors. "I'll see where Megan is."

"Megan's right here."

They all turned to see his beautiful ex-wife gliding toward them across the scruffy lawn.

He met her eyes. "François and Claudine gave me a lift in their Rover." He gestured toward the rowboat François had tied to a stake in the ground. "And a rowboat."

Megan offered her best smile to the elderly couple. "I'm Megan McLean," she said, as Claudine kissed her on each cheek. "Thank you for helping us out."

Claudine beamed her approval. "And thank you, my dear, for gracing our little island. It's been a very long time since our handsome neighbor had a suitable companion and I—"

"You must excuse my beloved wife." François stepped forward and kissed Megan's hand. "She sometimes speaks before she thinks."

"Listen," Jake broke in, feeling the way he had in the sinking rowboat, "Claudine and François brought champagne but it's after three. We should be getting back to the dock."

Megan's smile faded. "I thought the *Sea Goddess* didn't sail until eight o'clock."

Claudine clapped her hands together sharply. "None of this talk about leaving. We won't hear of it until we've toasted to Jake's success."

Megan's curiosity was piqued. "Jake's success?" She didn't mean to appear judgmental but playing piano on a yacht hardly called for a bottle of Perrier et Jouet.

"My dear, of course," Claudine cooed, linking her arm through Megan's. "When we first met him we certainly never thought he would come so far. His wife had just left him and—"

"Claudine," Jake warned, his tone grim, "Megan is my ex-wife."

The poor woman's face turned lobster red. "*Mon Dieu*, how I wish you had told me so."

Megan laughed. "Let's get some glasses from the kitchen, Claudine, and you can tell me all the terrible things Jake told you about his ex-wife."

"But there were no terrible things," Claudine sputtered. "He was heartbroken and—"

"The champagne glasses," François directed, shaking his head at his wife's volubility.

*Jake was heartbroken.* The thought intrigued Megan as she and Claudine headed toward the kitchen. Angry she would have believed. Out for blood. Sorry he'd ever gotten involved in the first place. But heartbroken? Not in a million years.

"About what you said out there," Megan began as she swung open the cupboards and took down four glasses for the champagne. "Was Jake—"

"Foolish talk from an old woman." Claudine mustered up a smile. "I spoke out of turn. You must forgive me."

"There's nothing to forgive," said Megan.

Claudine looked at her curiously. "You're even prettier than I'd imagined you to be."

"Thank you." This was the oddest conversation Megan had ever had.

"You and Jake would have made beautiful children together."

Jenny's adorable face seemed to materialize right there in front of Megan. "Well, I—I mean, maybe we..." Her words trailed off guiltily. She was relieved when François and Jake appeared in the doorway.

"The afternoon is waning," François announced in his quaintly accented English. "We must toast to Jake's success before he leaves for his—"

"This success," Megan said as Jake popped the cork. "I'm curious about—"

"They make too much of nothing," Jake interrupted. He looked downright embarrassed. "Playing piano isn't worth champagne."

"Modesty," said François. "With all of his—"

The champagne bottle hit the floor with a crash, followed by a string of oaths from Jake. "Clumsy sod." He brushed at his pants with the back of his hand. "So much for the toasts."

Claudine hurried off to find a towel while François bemoaned the loss of one of nature's wonders.

Megan eyed Jake. "I've never known you to be clumsy."

"My hands were wet," he said easily. "It happens."

"Yes," she said, unconvinced. "I imagine it does."

Both breathed a sigh of relief that their secrets would remain secret a little bit longer.

François and Claudine had never been much for celebrations that didn't include champagne. A few minutes later they said goodbye. Jake and Megan stood in the yard and watched as the Land Rover bumped its way back toward their side of the cove.

"Reality is tough for incurable romantics," Jake said as they turned back toward the cottage.

"They're sweet," Megan said. "Married so long and still in love with each other. They make it look so easy."

"It isn't. Life's dealt them some rough blows."

"Yes," Megan persisted, "but they're still together. What is it they know that we—" She stopped. "It's foolish to think about what might have been, isn't it?"

"Yeah," he said after a moment. Foolish but impossible to resist.

THEY SHARED THE PLUMS on the beach, watching the play of sunlight on the water and listening to the soft call of brightly colored birds high in the trees. The bittersweet mood lingered but there was something else at work there, a deeper understanding that ran counter to the ever-present current of sensuality.

"This is wonderful," Megan said as plum juice drizzled down her arm. "I should have served plums for lunch on the *Sea Goddess*. The contract would be in the bag." This was the decadent, voluptuous island experience everyone took a cruise to find.

He kissed her along the side of her mouth, drawing his tongue along the line of sticky juice. "You did great. You'll nail the contract."

"Feel free to put in a good word with the boss."

"You really want the franchise, don't you?"

"Of course I do," she said carefully.

"Somehow I never figured you for a working girl."

"Oh, you know how it is," she said, waving her hand in the air in a careless gesture. "Everyone has to do something."

A flip answer but she didn't dare handle it any other way. Today was for fantasy and she was determined to keep reality at bay for as long as she could.

This was a moment out of time, blessed with an unexpected ease and grace that neither had believed possible between them. He didn't say anything and neither did she. They didn't need to. He gathered her close. Her eyes were bright with tears as she lay her head against his shoulder. For the first time it wasn't heat that brought them together. It was the need to be close, to say with their bodies what they'd never been able to say with words.

He led her to a spot beneath a bower of tropical blooms, a spot where they were safe from prying eyes. Skin to skin. Heart to heart. They made love with passion and sweetness.

And with the knowledge that they were moving toward something that neither one of them knew how to handle.

"I hate to leave," Megan said as they gathered up their belongings, then placed them in the rowboat.

He looked at her, expecting to see the lie behind her words, but it wasn't there. "We could say to hell with the *Sea Goddess.*"

"And do what?" she asked with a laugh. "Row our way around the world?"

"Live dangerously, Meggie. You never know what's around the corner."

*A little girl,* she thought as he helped her into the rowboat. *The daughter I have to tell you about as soon as I find the courage.*

WHEN THEY PARTED company beneath an old mimosa tree in the center of town, Jake drew her into his arms and she went willingly.

"Tonight," Jake whispered.

Megan nodded, not trusting her voice.

Their kiss was so tender, so sweet, so unlike any they'd shared during their marriage that the last of her defenses crumbled at his feet. *Tell him,* her heart pleaded. *He has the right to know he has a child.* And, dear God, Jenny had the right to a father of her own.

She couldn't hide the truth from him any longer. Not if she wanted to look her daughter in the eye when she went home. Tonight when he came to her cabin she would tell him.

Jake vanished into the crowd. As part of the crew, he had things to do before they set sail again but Megan was free to enjoy La Mirada awhile longer. She'd noticed a shop at the far end of the street with a sign that boasted the finest selection of postcards in the Caribbean. Jenny adored postcards. Remembering her promise to send one from every port, Megan turned to head back to the store when she bumped smack into Val.

"If you're not all shopped out, why don't you join me?" Megan offered with a smile. "I'm on the great postcard hunt."

Val didn't return the smile. "Surprised you'd feel like wasting time with a commoner, all things considered."

"A commoner?" Megan's smile faltered. Val was looking at her as if she'd committed a crime. "What's wrong?"

"Nothing's wrong," Val said. "It's just I wouldn't have figured you for the type to sleep her way up the ladder."

Megan's back stiffened. "Would you care to explain that?"

"Oh, come on, honey. He's tall, he's gorgeous, he owns the company. You could do worse."

"Are you talking about Jake?"

Val nodded, one eyebrow arched. "Your ex and only."

Had the woman lost her mind? Megan laughed.

"Jake plays the piano, Val. I doubt if he even owns a rowboat."

Val reached into her straw bag and withdrew a folded copy of a St. Thomas newspaper. "Talk about luck." Val handed the paper to Megan. "Lie down with a piano player, wake up with a millionaire. It's the other way around for the rest of us mortals."

The story was right there on the front page. Eight column inches extolling the virtues of the Tropicale organization and their iconoclastic owners, Ian Macmillan and Jake Lockwood. If she had any doubts, the big black-and-white photograph of Jake erased them.

"Your hands are shaking." Val sounded surprised. "You really didn't know."

"No," Megan rasped over the pain in her chest. "I really didn't."

"At least now you can be sure you'll get the job."

"Not like this." Megan crumpled the paper into a ball. "I'd rather die." The taste of betrayal lay bitter on her tongue. Jake, her ex-husband, her renegade lover, had made his dreams come true...those same dreams that Megan had dismissed as the fantasies of a man who'd never amount to anything.

Suddenly it was all clear. The unexpected invitation to apply for the Tropicale contract. The request for Megan, and not Ingrid, to appear.

*The seduction.*

Her throat tightened and she took a deep breath, willing herself not to cry, not to let anyone see her pain.

She looked at Val. "How long until we set sail?"

Val checked her watch. "A little more than three hours."

"Good," said Megan. She'd be on a plane headed for home before he even knew she was gone.

And she would never, not ever, think of him again.

# Chapter Seven

Jake was in the office working on spec sheets for the *Sea Goddess*'s maiden voyage next month when Ian appeared in the doorway.

"I know I didn't do it," Ian said, "so that leaves you."

"I'm not in the mood for riddles," Jake muttered, marking his spot in the long column of numbers. "What are you talking about?"

"McLean," he answered, a wide grin on his face. "The cute little sheila who got under your skin. She's gone."

"Gone? What the hell do you mean, gone?"

"Gone as in out-of-here," Ian said, obviously enjoying Jake's confusion. "She bolted right before we sailed."

"Bull." This was payback time for the fight they'd had over Megan a few nights ago. He wouldn't give the guy the satisfaction.

"Sorry, mate. I saw her with my own eyes." He grinned. "She had a cab waiting on the dock."

Jake kicked back his chair. His pulse rate went into overdrive as he ran full-out toward Megan's cabin.

She'd be there. No reason why she wouldn't be. Ian was probably laughing his butt off, watching Jake make a fool of himself, but buried deep down inside him was a buzz of apprehension, that maybe, just maybe...

He banged on Megan's door. No answer. The buzz increased. He jiggled the handle. The door swung open and he stepped into the cabin. It took all of a nano-second to see that she was gone. It took another nano-second to see that she hadn't bothered to leave a note.

"So Cinderella really did fly the coop?"

He turned to see one of the female travel agents watching him from the doorway. The nametag on her left breast read Val.

"Is that a question or a statement?" He didn't have time for polite conversation.

Val peered into the cabin. "Looks like it's a fact." She eyed him with obvious interest. "Girl must've lost her mind. Most women would consider a guy like you the romantic equivalent of winning the lottery."

"Did she tell you where she was going?"

"*Moi?*" The travel agent dimpled. "Not hardly."

He returned her smile with a scowl. She didn't take the hint. "What the hell happened? Was there some kind of emergency?"

"Let's just say I made a teensy-tiny mistake." She looked up at him through tangled false lashes. "You're a naughty boy, Jake Lockwood. A girl likes to know when she's sleeping with the boss."

INGRID'S HOUSE WAS situated at the far end of a cul-de-sac in a solid, upper-middle-class Miami neighborhood that had escaped Hurricane Andrew's wrath the year before. Sprawling stucco ranch houses stood side-by-side with two-story English tudors. The lawns were lush and green, the perfect background for enormous beds of multicolored flowers of every variety. As beautiful as it was, it was the kind of neighborhood Megan would have sneered at when she lived in Palm Beach. Today she would consider herself blessed.

"You can pull in the driveway," Megan instructed the cabbie. "Right behind the Volvo." And next to the battered Ford Fiesta she called her own.

"Need help with your bags?" he asked after he unloaded them from the trunk.

She shook her head. "I can manage." She paid the bill, added a tip that made the driver frown, then started up the walk toward the front door. Thank God it was a weekday. Jenny would be in kindergarten until one o'clock. Megan doubted it, but maybe by then she'd have a grip on her emotions.

"What on earth?" Ingrid, clad in white shorts and a bright red maternity top, stood on the top step and stared at her in disbelief. "You're supposed to be in St. Thomas."

"Are you going to invite me in," Megan asked, stifling a yawn, "or do I have to get pushy about it?"

Ingrid stepped aside and ushered Megan into the cool, dim foyer. A basket of wildflowers rested on a plant stand near the staircase, a note of beauty and grace that described Ingrid perfectly.

"Look at you," said Megan, patting her friend's enormous belly. "You're even bigger than you were on Friday."

"And with good reason." Ingrid absently massaged the small of her back. "The doctor said any day now."

"I thought you had a couple of weeks."

"So did I but the baby has other ideas."

"So much for modern medicine. Babies still play by their own rules."

Ingrid nodded her agreement. "So what are you doing here, Megan? You're not supposed to be home for two more days."

"Nothing happened." Megan followed her into the sun-splashed kitchen. "I came home early. It's not against the law." Her voice caught on the last word. She prayed her friend didn't notice.

No such luck. Ingrid stopped dead in her tracks, blocking Megan's way. "Your ex?"

She nodded.

"Are you going to tell me about it or do I have to drag it out of you?"

"He owns Tropicale."

Ingrid looked at her, hesitated, then burst out laughing. "That's a good one, Megan. Now let's try the truth."

Megan stepped around her partner's considerable bulk, then claimed a chair at the kitchen table. "He owns Tropicale," she repeated. "Lock, stock and profits."

"I thought you said he was the piano player."

Megan rested her chin in her hands. "Apparently that charade was for my benefit."

"I can't believe this," said Ingrid, settling herself down onto a chair opposite Megan. "Do you suppose that's why The Movable Feast got the invitation?"

"Bingo, Sherlock. It wasn't our *remoulade*."

"When did he tell you?"

"He didn't."

"Who did?"

"A travel agent with a bad case of the hots for him." Megan's laugh was bitter. "Can you believe she accused me of sleeping my way to the top?"

"So what did he say when you confronted him?"

Megan felt her cheeks redden. "I didn't confront him."

"You've got to be kidding."

"Do I look like I'm kidding?"

"You look like you want me to shut up."

"But you're not going to, are you, Ingrid?"

"Not until I get some answers."

"I'm afraid I'm all out of answers."

Ingrid waited a moment then said, "Did you tell him about Jenny?"

"No." Megan met her partner's eyes. "And I'm glad I didn't."

"It seems to me you don't have the right to complain about Jake when you're as guilty as he is."

"What's that supposed to mean?"

Ingrid didn't flinch under Megan's flinty stare. "I think you know exactly what it means. Concealing the existence of a child is a lot more serious than hiding your bank balance."

"He's the one who set this whole thing in motion. Not me."

"I don't want to argue with you, Megan, but it doesn't matter who set it in motion. Jake is Jenny's father and you know where to find him. Do you really think you'll be able to look at your little girl and still keep them apart?''

IT DIDN'T TAKE LONG for word to get around the ship that Jake was one of Tropicale's owners. He barricaded himself in his office with a bottle of Scotch and set about getting roaring drunk. Unfortunately he'd never been good at getting drunk. Maybe it was because he was the child of a world-class drunk. Or maybe he'd been cursed with a cast-iron stomach. No matter how much he drank, or how quickly, he never quite managed to achieve that state of blissful numbness where all of your problems disappeared, if only temporarily.

There wasn't enough Scotch in the world to erase Megan from his mind. He knew that now for a fact. She was part of him, burned into his soul for eternity. He didn't like it. He'd pay the devil to change it. But there was nothing he could do about it.

''You blew it, mate.'' He slumped on the couch and took a slug straight from the bottle. He should have told her what he was about right from the start. How tough was it to say, ''I own the yacht. I own the company''? He didn't blame her for being angry. From her perspective it must have looked like he'd do anything to get her in bed, including lie.

And if he was being honest, he'd have to admit that's exactly what he'd done.

The chemistry between them had been so fierce, so hot, that he'd been powerless before the dark call of his blood.

"It's not over yet, Meggie," he vowed, taking another slug of Scotch. "Not by a long shot."

He'd let her walk out on him once before but this time was different. Whatever he'd done, however he'd hurt her, this time he wasn't going to let her go without a fight.

INGRID'S WORDS CAME back to haunt Megan later that evening.

She was giving Jenny her evening bath and shampoo, grateful to be settled again within the comforting embrace of routine. This was where she belonged. Safe in her tiny rented house with her little girl, the rest of the world an arm's length away.

"Okay, sweetie, close your eyes while I rinse your hair." She tested the spray against her arm then adjusted the cold water.

Jenny shook her head, sending shampoo bubbles flying. "Not yet."

Megan placed her hands on her hips and summoned up a frown. "I know what you're up to, young lady, and it's not going to work. Bedtime is still seven o'clock." This was an old battle and a familiar one.

Jenny's perfect little features slid into a scowl and for a moment the resemblance to Jake was so intense it stole Megan's breath away. "Courtney can stay up to watch 'The Simpsons' on Thursday and Danielle can watch 'Dinosaurs.'"

"We've been through this before, Jenny. Bedtime is seven o'clock in this house. No exceptions."

The little girl pouted while Megan rinsed her hair. Megan ignored her daughter's petulance and whistled one of the songs from *Beauty and the Beast* as she wrapped the child in a fluffy pink bath towel, then helped her out of the tub. It felt so wonderful to be home again that not even Jenny's mood could dim her happiness.

"If you put on your pajamas by yourself, I'll let you have some chocolate milk before you go to sleep."

"I don't want chocolate milk."

"You love chocolate milk."

Jenny fixed her with a look. "Kristin's daddy lets her play Nintendo until ten o'clock." The look sharpened. "If I had a daddy, he'd let me stay up and watch 'The Simpsons.'"

"Well, too bad for you," said Megan in a casual tone of voice. "You have a mommy and she says lights out at seven o'clock."

Jenny thrust her lower lip forward. "I don't like you anymore."

"I'm sorry to hear that but it doesn't change anything, Jenny."

"Daddies let you stay up as late as you want to."

*Oh God,* Megan groaned inwardly. *Why tonight?* For almost six years the "daddy" topic had been of little interest to Jenny and now, tonight, it was suddenly number one on her hit parade.

She sat down on the edge of the bathtub and rested her hands on the little girl's fragile shoulders. "Jenny, look at me." Jenny's gaze drifted to the window, to the door, then finally toward Megan. "Do you remember when we talked about why some families just have a mommy and some families just have a daddy?"

Jenny nodded her head. "Stace has a mommy and a daddy."

"Stace is a lucky little girl," Megan said, trying to keep her emotions in check. Staying with Ingrid and Miguel in their Norman Rockwellesque household was bound to stir up questions. It came with the territory. "I didn't have a mommy when I was a little girl."

Jenny's golden eyes widened. "Everybody has a mommy."

Megan shook her head. "My mother died when I was a baby."

"But you had a daddy, didn't you?"

"Yes, sweetheart, I had a daddy."

Jenny considered the situation. "Is your daddy staying with my daddy?"

*Please, God,* Megan begged again. *Help me answer this question and I'll never ask you for another thing as long as I live.*

She hugged Jenny close. "My daddy died just before you were born, sweetheart. Remember the pictures I showed you of your grandpa?"

"No." Jenny squirmed out of Megan's embrace. "Is my daddy dead too?"

*You're not listening, God. I need help and I need it fast!* "No, honey, your daddy isn't dead."

"Why doesn't he live here?"

Megan took a deep breath. "Remember how Mr. and Mrs. Dodd from next door stopped being married?"

"They got divorced," Jenny declared. "Lotsa parents get divorced."

For once Megan didn't correct Jenny's grasp of the

facts. "That's what happened to your daddy and me. We got divorced."

"Tiffany has two daddies and one mommy," she persisted. "And she's going to have a little brother but her mommy says she has to wait until Christmas until he's finished." Her eyes lit up with excitement. "Could I have a little brother for Christmas, too?"

Reproduction. At last an easy topic. She whispered her thanks. "Why don't we talk about it after you put your pajamas on, Jenny?"

"Can I still have chocolate milk before I go to sleep?"

She kissed the top of her daughter's head. "Of course you can."

Jenny threw her little arms around Megan and hugged her. "I missed you, Mommy. I don't like it when you go away."

"I missed you too." *More than you could ever imagine, Jen.*

"Can we have burritos for dinner tomorrow?"

"We sure can."

"Can I have a new Barbie for my birthday?"

"You'll find out on your birthday, honey."

"Am I gonna have a party?"

"Of course you're going to have a party."

"At Aunt Ingrid's?"

"At Aunt Ingrid's."

"Danielle had a clown at her birthday party."

"You'll have a super-duper party, Jenny. And the sooner you go to sleep the quicker the days will pass."

Jenny planted a squishy kiss on Megan's cheek. "You're the best mommy in the whole wide world."

Megan could only wonder how much longer she'd be able to hold on to the title.

EVERYONE AGREED the cruise was an unqualified success. The travel agents waxed enthusiastic about the *Sea Goddess* and all vowed to promote it heavily to prospective vacationers. The consensus was that Megan and The Movable Feast had provided the most innovative and delicious meals. It was also obvious that signing her up was highly unlikely.

"Good going, mate," Ian quipped as they watched the passengers disembark in Miami. "We lose our best prospect because you can't keep your trousers zipped. That sweet little Megan McLean was—" He never got to finish his sentence.

Jake hauled off and belted his partner in the jaw. Ian got in a quick shot to Jake's right eye but Jake quickly recovered and landed a left-right combination that knocked Ian on his butt.

Later on Jake blamed it on the fact that he was tired and hung over, but the truth was he'd had a taste for blood that wouldn't be denied. He was filled with anger, and loss, and a score of conflicting emotions, most of which he'd spent a lifetime avoiding. And the best way he could think of to dispel those emotions was by using his fists. Primitive? He wouldn't argue that. But it was still damn effective.

He helped Ian to his feet. "Your jaw's swelling."

Ian touched it and winced. "Second time in five days. Either we start using gloves or I'm going to hire a bodyguard."

"It was nothing personal," Jake offered by way of apology.

Ian looked at him sharply and grinned. "You're going to have one hell of a black eye."

Somehow that prospect made Jake even happier than it made his partner.

TRY AS SHE MIGHT, Megan found it difficult to accept the old boundaries. In less than a week her entire life had been turned on its ear and no matter how hard she tried, she couldn't set it right. Oh, it felt wonderful to be home again with Jenny but not even the deep pleasure of motherhood could alter the fact that she wanted more. Needed more.

She missed his sound and his smell, the warmth of his body against hers at night, the feeling that the one man on earth who was all wrong for her was the only man she would ever love.

That thought was enough to send her under the bedcovers permanently.

She'd loved him once but she didn't any longer. You had to trust a man in order to love him and Megan doubted if she would trust another man again as long as she lived. Her father had been the most important man in her life and he hadn't cared enough about her or the grandchild she'd carried to protect their future. There was no reason to believe that Jake would be any different.

And she wasn't about to risk Jenny's heart—or her own—to find out.

JAKE RARELY SPENT time in Tropicale's Miami offices but this time he was in no hurry to return to the west coast.

His assistant knocked, then stepped into his office. "I'm sorry, Mr. Lockwood, but Ms. McLean still won't take your calls."

Jake scowled. "What do you mean she won't take my calls?"

Helen tugged at the sleeve of her white blouse. "She doesn't want to talk to you."

"Did you tell her she got the contract?"

Poor Helen shifted position, the toe of her black pump digging deeper into the carpet. "She said she doesn't want the contract."

Jake let out a string of Aussie expletives that turned Helen's cheeks a vivid shade of pink. He considered himself an almost-American but, when it came to cursing, there was nothing like the mother tongue. His poor assistant, however, looked as if she was about to faint.

"Sorry, Helen," he said, breaking a pencil in half, then tossing it across the room.

Helen nodded, the color in her cheeks fading somewhat. "Maybe you should call her yourself, Mr. Lockwood. You might have more luck."

Jake shook his head. It would take more than luck to budge the stubborn Ms. McLean. When Megan made up her mind to something, a herd of wild elephants couldn't knock her off course. It was nice to know some things hadn't changed.

"Should I call Celia Briscoe and tell her she got the contract?"

"Hell, no. The Movable Feast won fair and square."

"If you'll excuse my saying so, Mr. Lockwood, it doesn't matter how The Movable Feast won the contract if they won't sign on the dotted line."

Leave it to Helen to zero in on the heart of the matter. "They'll sign."

"Ms. McLean won't even talk to you on the phone. I find it hard to believe she'll sign a contract with you."

"She'll sign." He rummaged through a pile of papers on his desk. "Do we have an address on Movable Feast?"

"They use a post office box." Helen thought for a moment. "But I do seem to remember a street address on one of the waivers we had them sign for the insurance company. That must be their office address."

"Get it for me," Jake barked. "And have three copies of the contract ready in ten minutes."

Helen's eyes widened. "You're going to show up at their kitchen with the contracts?"

"Whatever works."

"There *are* other caterers, Mr. Lockwood. Ones that you can actually get hold of. Celia Briscoe—"

"Just get the contracts ready. I'll take care of the rest."

"I CAN'T BELIEVE this." Megan rooted through the back of her car and came up empty again. "What kind of mother would leave her child's birthday present at home?"

"A busy one," said Ingrid, massaging the small of

her back. "I'm surprised you managed to finish the cake." She sighed loudly. "I wish I could've been more help with the party, but…" Her voice trailed off.

"Good grief, Ingrid. Offering up your house for this shindig is more than enough."

Ingrid grinned. "You do realize I'll get my own back when you take care of Stace for us while I'm in the hospital."

"Stace is a doll. We love having her around." Megan climbed behind the wheel. "I'll be back as fast as I can. The girl with the pony should be here any minute." She started the engine, then checked the rearview mirror. "Tell Miguel I'll be forever in his debt if he'll film Jenny and—"

"Go get the present," Ingrid ordered. "We'll take care of everything else."

"DAMN IT," Jake swore as he turned down yet another rundown residential street. He'd been driving around for twenty minutes and he had yet to find 56 Tecumseh Avenue. In fact he was beginning to doubt there even was a Tecumseh Avenue.

The address had to be wrong. He looked around at the tiny houses with their parched lawns and old cars crowding the driveways. Megan wouldn't be caught dead driving through a neighborhood like this, much less working here.

He'd noticed a gas station about a mile back. Maybe somebody there would be able to tell him where he'd gone wrong. He was about to make a U-turn in someone's driveway when he caught a glimpse of a street sign that was hanging by one bolt. T UM EH. Tecumseh. It had to be. He swung a quick right onto the narrow street and peered at the house numbers.

Number 56 was a tiny cottage, not much bigger than the one he owned on La Mirada. Someone had carefully painted it a pale yellow with crisp white trim. Flower boxes, heavy with red blooms, were at each window. A little Ford wagon that had seen better days idled in the driveway. Megan here? Not bloody likely.

He braked to a stop in front of the house and turned off the engine. Still it wouldn't hurt to check.

JENNY'S BIRTHDAY present was in the toolshed, hidden behind the grass catcher, right where Megan had left it. The toolshed was the only place she could be certain Jenny wouldn't look because she might run into spiders.

Megan dusted a fine layer of grass clippings off the brightly wrapped package, adjusted the bow, then ran back into the house for her sunglasses. She was debating the wisdom of locking the kitchen window when the telephone rang.

"Better come back right away," said Ingrid. "I think I'm in labor."

"Good grief, Ingrid, you're kidding!"

"I never kid about labor. Hurry up, Meg."

She popped on her sunglasses, grabbed the birthday present, then hurried toward the front door as footsteps crunched their way up the walkway. The UPS woman, maybe. Or a FedEx delivery. She'd ordered some twenty-quart stockpots a few weeks back. It would be nice if the darned things arrived before the big Cooper-Hardison wedding next month. If they didn't, she'd be making clear consommé for three hundred in metal washtubs.

"I'm in a rush," she called out as she swung open the door. "If there's anything for me to sing, I'll—"

She stopped. It wasn't UPS or FedEx or the U.S. mail.

It was Jake.

And he was looking for a fight.

## Chapter Eight

The thing to do was act cool even though her hands were shaking. If Jake had shown up an hour earlier, he would have been standing right there at the foot of the walkway staring at his daughter. Megan whispered a quick prayer of thanks for good friends and birthday parties.

Head high, she stepped out onto the rickety porch. He had a black eye, she noted. Her only regret was that she wasn't the one who'd given it to him. "What are you doing here?"

"What the hell do you think I'm doing here?"

"I'm not in the mood for questions, Jake. Just tell me what you want, then leave."

"What if I don't, Megan?" He stepped closer. "What'll you do, run away?"

"I have this thing about liars," she said smoothly. "Can't help myself. I just automatically run in the opposite direction."

"Not this time," he said.

In a blink of an eye he was standing on the step in front of her and she was in his arms.

"Jake, I—"

His kiss was angry. So was her response. A ferocious mating of will and desire that left her breathless and enraged.

He broke the kiss but not the hold he had on her arms.

Her eyes widened but she didn't give an inch. "We're going to talk," he said.

"The hell we are." She wanted to storm off but he held her tight.

"You know I own Tropicale, don't you?"

"Remind me to send Val some flowers. If it hadn't been for her, I'd still think you were a lowly piano player."

"I was going to tell you, Meggie. That night."

"Right," she said with a bitter laugh. "After you got what you wanted between the sheets."

"There's more to it than that."

"Sure there is." Her voice broke but she recovered quickly. "If you don't leave in the next thirty seconds, I'll call the police."

"Not if I don't let you."

"You don't scare me."

"No?" His eyes glittered with dark fire. "Then you're not paying attention. We're going to talk if I have to tie you up and lock you in a room."

"Big talk from a man who gets his kicks slumming with the masses. Now I know how you got the black eye."

"*Who's* slumming?" he asked, ignoring the comment about his eye. "This isn't exactly the Ritz-Carlton you're visiting."

She took a deep breath. "I'm not visiting."

"Your partner's place?"

She shook her head.

He looked skeptical. "I get it. This is where you do your cooking."

"Wrong again." She glanced at her watch. "Ten seconds, Jake, then I'm calling the police. You're not welcome here."

"You're not planning to stay here all night, are you?"

She lifted her chin. "So what if I am?"

"This is a lousy neighborhood. It probably gets lousier after dark."

"This is a terrific neighborhood," she shot back. "Too bad it isn't fancy enough for your nouveau riche tastes."

AN ALTERNATE UNIVERSE, that's what it was. The real Megan McLean wouldn't say something like that.

"Since when did you become a populist?" Jake remembered the girl who thought anything south of Palm Beach was swampland fit only for gators and rednecks. He released his hold on her. "You must be counting the minutes until you can run home."

"Go away," she said, poking her finger into his chest. The look in her eyes was fierce. "Why don't you go back to Australia and chase kangaroos?"

"Come with me to Australia," he said, ignoring the way her hands were clenched into fists. "Let me show you where I grew up."

"I don't give a damn where you grew up." She shoved him in the general direction of the street. "I just want you to leave."

"Sign the contract with Tropicale and I'll leave."

"I'd rather be dead."

"Don't push me," he growled. "Now let's go back to your place and straighten this whole thing out."

"This *is* my place."

"You can do better than that."

"Damn you. I *am* telling the truth." The fire in her eyes was softened by the sheen of unshed tears.

"You live here?"

"I live here."

"What about the house in Palm Beach?" Her father's pink palace where the beautiful princess lived in splendor.

"There is no house in Palm Beach."

"You sold it?"

"Don't I wish." Her laughter sounded false. "The bank and two mortgage companies relieved me of that particular burden."

"You're telling me your father's insurance didn't cover it?"

She looked as if she'd rather walk across a bed of hot coals than answer his questions. "There was no insurance, Jake." She met his eyes. "No insurance. No stocks. No bonds. Nothing."

"With all his money?" Jake tried to fathom her expression. "Look, I was no fan of your father's, but he wasn't that old. He probably didn't think—"

"You don't get it, do you?" she asked, her voice rising. "My father didn't just die, Jake. He killed himself. He walked straight out into the ocean and he never came back." She looked away for a moment. "And he didn't give a damn if I died right along with him." Darrin McLean had gambled away his assets on slow horses and fast women, and when it all became too much he took the easy—and permanent—way out.

His gut burned with rage. "That son of a bitch threw you to the wolves."

She didn't deny it. She didn't do anything at all, except meet his gaze head-on. For the first time he understood the shadow of vulnerability he'd seen in her eyes. It hadn't been his imagination. It had been real. All too real.

"I don't want you living like this," he said. "I can help you to—"

"I don't need your charity and I don't particularly want your company." Her voice shook with anger. "Now if you'll excuse me, I was on my way out."

"We're not finished."

"Oh yes, we are."

"I screwed up," he roared. "I admit it. I should've told you right up front that I owned the company."

"Get out of my way," she said. "I don't want to see your face ever again."

"Grow up, Meggie." His temper flared. "If you'd stop running and start listening, we might be able to work this out."

"Work what out? There's nothing to work out." She shoved him again, harder this time. "You mean nothing to me, Jake. All you are is a mistake I'd rather forget."

He grabbed her by the shoulders and pulled her body up against his.

"Jake, if you—"

"Shut up." His mouth slanted across hers hungrily.

Her lips parted in surprise. He took full advantage of her moment of weakness as his hands cupped the heavy fullness of her breasts.

"I despise you," she said, breaking the kiss. "Only a bastard would take advantage of the situation."

"Only a fool would let it pass."

"Go ahead," she taunted him. "Show me what a big man you are. There's nothing I can do to stop you."

"You're right. If I wanted to take you right here in your front yard, there's not one damn thing you could do to stop me. But that's not what I want and you know it."

"I pity you." She pulled away from his grasp. "You don't have any idea about what's important in life."

"And you do?" He laughed. "I saw you on the cruise, Megan. You were desperate to land the franchise." He gestured toward the house. "Now I know why. You're counting the days until you're back in Palm Beach where you belong."

"You don't know what you're talking about."

"The hell I don't."

"I'm not—" She stopped. "Forget it. This conversation is pointless." She started for her car. "Follow me," she yelled over her shoulder, "and I swear I'll have you arrested."

She climbed into the car and started the engine. Her hands shook so badly she could barely hold the steering wheel. *Take a deep breath,* she ordered herself. Gunning the engine, she roared out of the driveway and zoomed down the street.

Jake followed in hot pursuit.

For a while it seemed as if she'd have to drive all the way to Key West. For ten minutes she zigzagged through traffic, heading south, attempting to lose him. But when she checked the rearview mirror around every turn, there he was, still dogging her. She was desperate. If she had to, she would drive off a bridge. There was no way on earth she would lead him to Jenny.

She finally ditched him forty minutes later. A quick right, a sharp left, then a ridiculous race through a parking lot and she was free. Badly shaken, she pulled off to the side of the road and burst into tears of relief.

*This can't be happening,* she thought as she started once again for Ingrid's house and her daughter's birthday party. Jake wasn't supposed to show up on her doorstep, demanding apologies and explanations, drawing responses from her that she'd sell her soul to the devil not to feel.

She wanted to grab Jenny and run. California, maybe. Or Seattle. Some little town in the middle of Montana where Jake could never find them. He was too wild, too unpredictable. He knew nothing about being part of a family—and he cared even less.

She'd spent much of her life looking for a hero, but there were no heroes any longer. Maybe there never had been. A long long time ago she had believed her father would move mountains to keep her safe from harm. Discovering the truth made her question everything she'd believed as a child. Everything she'd considered important as a young woman.

That wasn't going to happen to Jenny. Not as long

as there was breath in her body. If it meant they had to pull up stakes and move to another city, then so be it. Jake's attention span had never been very good. He had other things to think about besides tormenting his ex-wife, and sooner or later she would fade back into memory.

Ingrid wouldn't mind if she and Jenny stayed with her for a night or two, just long enough for Megan to decide what to do next.

With a little luck, Jake would climb back on board his boat and sail out of her life forever.

She drove the rest of the way to Ingrid's house with one eye on the road and the other on the rearview mirror, but there was no sign of Jake. Thank God. She was able to plaster a fairly normal smile on her face as she pulled into the driveway.

The horse trailer from Rent-A-Pony was parked in front of the house. She wished she'd seen Jenny's face when Sparkles arrived but she consoled herself that there would be other birthdays. The wonderful sound of children's laughter floated toward her from the backyard and, despite everything, she smiled as Jenny's sweet voice rose above the others.

This was what it was all about. The pain and heartache. The loneliness and the hard work. It had nothing to do with five-bedroom houses and fancy cars...or a man who would break her heart in two. Her daughter's happiness meant the world to her and she'd been crazy to believe she needed anything else—or anyone—to make her life complete.

She was smiling as she crossed the lawn and headed around the side of the enormous two-story house.

"I'm back, Ingrid!" she called out. "Grab a lemonade and put your feet up because—"

"Oh, thank God you're here!" A young girl Megan recognized as one of Ingrid's neighbors popped up at her side. She had the camcorder clutched in her hands. "You wouldn't *believe* what happened." Her face wrinkled comically. "It was really gross. Mrs. Chavez's water broke right there on the patio. I was really scared the baby was just gonna pop right out near the barbecue pit."

"Ingrid's having the baby?"

The girl nodded vigorously. "Mr. Chavez cleaned up the gunk and they went off to the hospital. My mom and me said we'd watch the kids until you got back."

Megan looked over to the laughing knot of little girls who were waiting for the chance to ride Sparkles, the Happy Birthday Pony. Jenny was right in the thick of things. "They don't look any the worse for the wear." She looked back at the teenager. "How did you handle their questions?"

"There weren't any," said the girl with a shrug. "Sparkles showed up and ponies are a lot more interesting than babies."

Megan counted her blessings. She was all in favor of telling kids the truth about the facts of life, but six seemed a little young to explain the wonders of the amniotic sac. She took the camcorder from the girl.

"Thanks for your help," she said. "I can take over from here."

"I don't mind," said the girl. "I was kinda hoping

to get a ride on Sparkles myself." She gave Megan a sheepish look. "If you don't mind, that is."

Megan laughed. "Don't let me stop you. If Sparkles doesn't have any objections, then it's okay with me."

With a whoop of excitement the young girl practically galloped across the yard to wait her turn.

Megan looked at the camcorder with dismay. It didn't look all that difficult to use. She'd tried her hand at it last Christmas when Ingrid and Miguel wanted a family record of opening presents beneath the tree.

"First the lens cap comes off," she muttered. "Then you check the light meter."

"Tape," said a familiar voice behind her. "Make sure you have enough tape."

*God, no. Please not now...not here.*

"Great driving, Meggie," he said in that infuriatingly sexy Aussie voice of his. "If I didn't know better, I'd think you were trying to get away from me."

"I *was* trying to get away from you."

He gestured toward the kids waiting for their turn to ride Sparkles. "Since when did you go into the baby-sitting business?"

She felt light-headed with fear. "This is my partner's house."

"She has one hell of a big family."

"It's a birthday party, you fool," she snapped, spinning around to glare up at him.

"So where is your partner? I'd like to meet the money behind your operation before you sign on the dotted line."

"I'm not signing on the dotted line. You can take your contract and—"

"That temper of yours always did get you into trouble, Meggie. How does your partner like it when you run away at the first sign of rough weather? That's not going to get you back to Palm Beach."

She didn't look at him. She didn't acknowledge his words. Turning on her heel she headed for the patio telephone.

"If you're calling for pizza, make mine pepperoni," he drawled, following close behind.

"I'm calling the police," she snapped. "This is harassment and I won't stand for it."

"The Miami police force has enough to worry about. Don't waste their time."

"The hell I won't." She grabbed for the phone but he got there first. "So help me, Jake, I'll—"

"I'm leaving in a few days," he said without preamble. "It's now or never. Come with me, Meggie. We'll work it out while we see the world. We have another ship ready to sail out of Bermuda. Then I'm flying to Hawaii and—"

"I don't give a damn about your itinerary." She glared up at him, praying her fear didn't show. Praying that Jenny would remain occupied with the pony. Praying that this was all a bad dream and she would wake up in her own bed, with Jenny safe and sound in the next room. "I'll give you ten seconds to get out of here."

He handed her the phone. "You might as well call the police then, Meggie, because I'm not going anywhere until we talk this out."

To her horror, tears welled in her eyes. "Go away,"

she managed, her voice breaking. "I don't need you or anyone else."

He grabbed her by the arms and shook her. "You might be able to get someone else to believe that, but not me. What are you hiding, Meggie? What the hell's going on?"

And then it happened. The worst of her fears was realized. From across the yard Jenny let out a shriek and barreled full speed across the grass toward them.

"You let my mommy alone!" she yelled, heading straight for Jake. "Don't touch my mommy!"

# Chapter Nine

"What the hell—" Before he could spit out the words, the tiny bundle of fury tackled him around the knees. From the patio, he looked up at Megan, whose face had gone pale. "Who is she?" he asked.

"Go away!" the child shrieked. "You can't touch my mommy."

He stood up and held off the little demon. "I'm not touching anyone's mommy." The kid must have been out in the sun too long.

She looked up at him with fierce golden eyes and a stab of something damn close to fear shot through his chest. "I saw you! You pushed her and I hate you!" With that the pint-size pugilist hauled off and punched him in the thigh.

"Jenny." Megan placed a hand atop the child's head. "Everything is fine. Apologize to Mr. Lockwood for hitting him."

The kid looked as if she'd like to bite him in the leg. The feeling was mutual.

"No," she snapped, her lower lip protruding. "You can't make me. It's my birthday."

That tone of voice...the way her little jaw was set

in granite. Recognition was hovering just beyond reach. He hoped it stayed there.

"Forget it, Megan," he said. "She didn't draw blood."

Megan nodded. A small muscle in her cheek worked furiously.

*No,* he thought. *I don't want to know this.*

The little girl looked up at him. "You talk funny."

He looked down at her. "So do you."

"I do not. I talk normal."

"So do I."

"Uh-unh." She shook her head and her silky hair brushed against her cheeks. "You talk like Croco—" She stopped.

"Crocodile Dundee," said Megan, her voice a whisper. "It's her favorite movie."

"What's your name?" he asked.

"I can't talk to strangers."

"He's not a stranger, Jenny." Megan was trembling. "He's an...an old friend of mine."

"I'm Jenny," the kid said. "Who are you?"

"Jake." He squatted down in front of her.

Those eyes.... Damn it. Where had he seen eyes like that before?

"You have good ears, Jenny. Crocodile Dundee is from Australia. So am I."

"I have a stuffed kangaroo in my room," Jenny asserted, looking at him with a mixture of dislike and curiosity. "I keep pennies in her pouch."

"How does the kangaroo feel about that?"

Jenny sighed broadly. "The kangaroo isn't *real*."

Megan placed her hand on the child's shoulder.

"The pony won't be here much longer, Jenny. Why don't you go and have one last ride before Sparkles leaves."

The little girl was gone in a flash leaving Jake alone with a woman he thought he knew.

"Her birthday?"

Megan nodded.

Six years...six long years. He'd been a fool to believe life could stand still. "She's yours, isn't she?"

The expression on her face was one of sadness and wonder. "Yes."

The question burned his gut, tore its way up through his chest, ripped at his throat. Some other man had lain between her legs, joined his body with hers, and made that little girl with the red hair and fierce temper. Some other man had seen the look of passion in her eyes, the look that he'd remembered through six long years of emptiness without her. The existence of a child paled beside the reality of another man.

For one terrible moment he wanted to wrap his hands around her throat and squeeze until she collapsed limp in his arms, the memory of other men erased forever from her mind. But it wouldn't be enough. He wouldn't be able to erase the truth from his heart.

MEGAN SAW IT IN HIS FACE. His jaw was set in granite. His mouth was tight with barely controlled anger. The look in his eyes was one of betrayal and regret.

*He doesn't know,* she thought in amazement. He'd looked at Jenny and he hadn't realized the truth. A towering anger rose inside her chest, an anger that matched his.

"You don't see it, do you?" she asked. "My God, Jake, are you blind?" She pointed toward Jenny who was jumping up and down as she waited her turn on the pony. "Look at her. Take a good long look at her and tell me what you see."

He looked toward the child with the red hair and golden eyes. That sense of recognition he'd experienced a few minutes ago returned, stronger this time. The child was laughing about something, her eyes crinkling at the outer corners.

The same way his eyes crinkled when he—

A dark, fierce emotion rose up from the deepest part of his soul, blocking out the sun. He turned toward Megan. "She's mine." A statement, not a question, for the truth hammered inside his chest.

She nodded.

He went to grab her by the arm but the memory of that fierce little girl stopped him in his tracks. His daughter? "When the hell were you going to tell me, Megan? When she turned twenty-one?"

"Never," she snapped. "If I had my way, you'd never have known about her."

"You don't think I had the right to know I was a father?"

"You weren't around, Jake. I couldn't tell you."

He didn't want logic. "What does she know about me?"

"Nothing."

"She thinks I'm dead?"

"No. Jenny knows we're divorced. There are a lot

of single parent families out there these days, Jake, in case you haven't noticed. We've done just fine on our own and we'll continue to do just fine.''

He grabbed her arm and pulled her behind a huge rhododendron bush. ''Not this time, Megan. You're not calling the shots again.'' She'd walked out on him twice. He wasn't going to let it happen a third time.

''Take your hands off me. You have no say in this, Jake. None.''

''The hell I don't.'' He wanted to shake her until her teeth rattled but he wasn't sure he could stop if he did.

''You're hurting me.''

''You're lucky I don't kill you.''

Her face contorted as she fought tears. He used to be a sucker for women in tears but now he didn't know how he felt about anything. A scrap of conversation came back to him and he reached out and grabbed it. ''You said you tried to call me after your father died.'' He gestured toward Jenny who was giggling as a young woman led the pony around the yard. ''Is that why?''

Megan nodded.

''Why didn't you keep trying?''

Her eyes flashed fire. ''Detectives cost money, Jake. I was too busy worrying about keeping a roof over my daughter's head to spend it chasing a dream.''

That look of vulnerability he'd noticed on the *Sea Goddess*...the soft uncertainty in her eyes. He hadn't imagined any of it. She'd walked through the fire and been made stronger by it and he found his rage battling with profound respect for all she had accomplished.

"You didn't have to give birth to her," he said, pushing for answers.

"Yes, I did," she replied, wiping her eyes with the back of her hand. "I loved her from the first second I knew about her."

He was at a loss to understand the primal emotions she talked about. That fierce maternal bond that began long before the child was born. All he felt was a bewildering sense of shock.

"You were dead broke. How the hell did you think you were going to take care of her?"

"I didn't think. I just *felt*." She'd hocked her jewelry first thing and lived off the proceeds while the bones of her father's life were picked clean by creditors. "I don't think I would have survived if it hadn't been for the baby. Knowing there was a reason to get up each morning got me through the worst of it."

"What about your medical bills?"

Her eyes flashed with fire but she answered his question. "I worked as a receptionist in a health club. Fortunately they catered to mothers-to-be and I was a walking advertisement." The health benefits had picked up the obstetrician's bill and some of the hospital stay.

"And after she was born?"

"I found a way. The first moment I saw her I knew I'd do anything for her." She looked at him. "But you just don't get any of this, do you?"

He thought of his own life. The arid expanse of his childhood. His wandering teens. The years ruled by ambition at the expense of love. "No," he said. "Not one bloody bit of it."

"Then go. You're not looking to be a father, Jake, and I don't want you to be one."

"You've made enough decisions for me. It's my turn now."

His words hit her like a slap in the face.

"Look at her," she said, unable to mask the emotion in her voice. "She doesn't need any confusion. She doesn't need anything but me."

He started to speak when Megan turned suddenly and made for the circle of children at a dead run.

"What the hell?" He hadn't heard or seen anything out of the ordinary but she'd reacted as if she'd heard a warning siren go off.

By the time he joined them the crisis was past. Megan held a little blond girl in her arms while Jenny glowered at the two of them. It wasn't hard to fill in the blanks.

"Apologize this minute, Jennifer." Megan's tone brooked no nonsense.

Jenny's stubborn little chin grew more stubborn before his eyes. "No."

"Into the house, young lady." Megan pointed toward the back door. "Go up to the guest room and think about what you've done. When you're ready to apologize you can come back down."

He watched as Jenny stormed across the lawn, muttering dark threats under her breath. She had his temper and Megan's stubbornness and the combination was as explosive as a hand grenade.

Against his better judgment he fell into step with her. "So what did you do back there?"

"Stace is a big crybaby," Jenny said. "I wanted to ride the pony and she wouldn't let me."

"Maybe it was her turn."

"It wasn't her turn. It was my turn." She looked up at him, her small face a portrait of righteous fury. "It's my birthday and I get to do what I want."

"Birthdays don't give you the right to hurt people."

"I don't like you. You're not nice to children."

"Neither are you."

Her brows drew together in a frown that was so purely Megan that his heart seemed to slam against his rib cage in recognition. "But that's okay. I am a children."

"Being a grown-up doesn't mean you can be cruel to other grown-ups." At least not in a more perfect world than the one in which they lived.

She considered him thoughtfully, her big golden eyes—*his* eyes—serious. "Do you have a kangaroo?"

Where did that question come from? It took him a moment to shift gears. "If you apologize to your friend I'll tell you about the kangaroo who lived in my backyard."

"No," she said. "Stace is dumb." A sly look crossed her face. "You're dumb, too."

With that she ran into the house and slammed the door behind her. *That's my daughter,* he thought, *and I don't even like her.*

And what was worse, the feeling was mutual.

SPARKLES THE PONY left not long after Jenny was banished to the house to think about her transgressions. Her absence put a bit of a damper on the party but

Megan called on every trick in the book to keep the kids occupied and happy.

Miguel called once to say that, to everyone's surprise, Ingrid's labor looked to be a long one. "Don't worry," Megan soothed. "Everything's fine here. Just give Ingrid my love."

"Why is it taking so long?" Stace asked, her blue eyes wide. "Mommy said the baby comes down the slide from her tummy. It only takes me a second to slide down a slide."

"Well, it's not quite a slide, honey." Megan was acutely aware of Jake's presence. "Your mommy and the baby have to work very hard to make it happen. That's why they call it labor."

A little girl named Patrice piped up. "My daddy said Mommy called him a stinking son of a—"

"Why don't we play a game of statues?" Megan broke in, and not a minute too soon.

They stared at her as if she were speaking in tongues.

"What's that?" asked Stace.

"We never heard of that game," added another child.

Jake, who'd been watching the whole thing with unnerving intensity, stepped forward. "I know a story."

The children turned en masse to look at Jake, and Megan was once again reminded of how flirtatious little girls could be. If she didn't know better she'd swear she heard the sound of Cupid's arrow piercing a dozen tiny hearts.

"That's very nice of you," she said formally, "but I'm sure you have to leave."

"No, I don't."

"Yes, you do."

"I'm not going anywhere, Meggie."

The little girls listened with rapt attention.

Megan lowered her voice. "Don't do this to me, Jake."

He turned toward the girls. "I'm not good at telling fairy tales," he said, offering a dazzling smile, "but I can tell you all about Australia."

Jenny must have been watching from an upstairs window because a few minutes later Megan noticed her daughter standing near one of Ingrid's favorite orange trees. Jake was telling a funny story about shearing an unwilling sheep. All of the little girls were laughing.

All of them except Jenny.

APPARENTLY THE SECRET to talking with children was to concentrate on kangaroos and Crocodile Dundee. Jake told his joey-in-the-yard story five times and still the little girls clamored for more.

"Do koala bears really smell like cough drops?" asked Stace.

Jake grinned. "You'd smell like cough drops, too, if all you ate were eucalyptus leaves."

He glanced toward Jennifer who sat by herself under an orange tree, playing with one of those platinum blond dolls with centerfold bodies. She was going out of her way to make it obvious that she had no interest in kangaroos or sheepshearing, although she did glance up when he described a real-life Crocodile Dundee he'd met in Tasmania. There was a brittleness in the way she held herself, the obvious posture of a child desperate to join her friends but unwilling to compromise her pride.

There was no doubt that Jennifer was his daughter and Megan's. It was there in the set of her jaw, the line of her shoulders, the eyes that were as familiar to him as his own in the mirror each morning. He already knew the girl had Megan's stubborn streak and his own quicksilver temper. She loved her mother and didn't trust him one bit and he was glad of it. The last thing he wanted was a little girl looking up at him with trusting eyes, as if he were the hero in one of her picture books.

He'd never wanted to be anyone's hero. Or anyone's father, for that matter. A child was better off with no father than one who was all wrong for the job. He knew that better than most people.

He shook his head, trying to forestall the memories. His daughter was looking at him, her small features set in lines of pure stubbornness. But it was her eyes that drew him in. His eyes. His temper. His insecurities.

If push came to shove, he wasn't convinced he'd ever be able to make the right decision where she was concerned and he had the feeling she knew that as well as he did.

*Don't look at me like that,* he thought, meeting her eyes. *I don't want to change your life.* There was nothing he could offer her that could surpass the love Me-

gan gave so freely. And he knew why there could be
no room in Megan's life for him.

"OKAY, EVERYONE," Megan called as she placed the
birthday cake on the picnic table in the center of the
yard. "Gather around while Jenny blows out the candles."

Jenny, cheeks pink with excitement, climbed up on
one of the benches and leaned over. "Do I get to make
a wish?"

Megan gave her a hug. "As many as you want."

Jenny took a deep breath, then blew out all of the
candles on the very first try.

"Now my wishes come true, don't they?" she
asked Megan as she leapt down from the bench.

The words caught in Megan's throat. Jake stood a
few feet behind Jenny, watching the proceedings. The
expression in his eyes was unreadable but his inten-
tions were clear. No matter how unwelcome she made
him feel, he wasn't about to leave until he was good
and ready.

*Go away,* Megan thought fiercely as she dished out
ice cream and cake to the little girls. *You don't belong
here.* He didn't have the right to stand there as if he
were part of their lives, making her feel things she
didn't want to feel. Couldn't he see what he was doing, the chance he was taking? The last thing she
wanted was for Jenny to see him as her knight in shining armor.

By the time the little girls had been served and were
seated around the folding tables set out on the lawn,
Megan was ready to strangle him.

"Help yourself to some cake," she said dryly.

"Don't mind if I do." He cut himself a huge slice and placed it on a paper plate. "How about you?"

"I lost my appetite."

"This moral outrage of yours is getting old, Megan. I'm the one who just found out he has a kid."

"There's no point going over this again," Megan muttered, aware of Jenny's curious glance. "You know now." She paused for effect. "Same as I know about Tropicale."

"There's a big difference between hiding a kid and hiding a company."

"I didn't hide Jenny."

"The hell you didn't."

The last of her self-control snapped. "What exactly do you want from all of this, Jake? If you're even thinking of playing daddy at this late date, so help me I'll—"

"I don't want to be her father," he said bluntly.

She hated herself for the disappointment his words evoked. "Then we're in agreement," she said, forcing her voice to remain even. "You don't want to be part of Jenny's life and I don't want you to be."

"You have it all figured out, don't you? Blow my life out of the water and leave me behind, wondering what in hell happened."

"I didn't want you to know about her. This wasn't supposed to happen."

"None of this was supposed to happen." He'd wanted to get her out of his system. See her one more time and put the past to rest. He hadn't expected to want her the way he did. He hadn't expected that sleeping with her again would make his desire for her grow stronger. Yeah, he knew all about things that weren't supposed to happen.

"Just go," she pleaded, a quaver in her voice. "Go wherever it is you were going to go and forget we even exist. We've been doing fine up until now without you."

"You're living in a lousy neighborhood. Your clothes are out of style and you're driving a car that's older than our kid. You're drowning, Megan, and I'm the only one who can help you."

"We don't need your help."

"Give me a day with her and you won't see me again." He'd care for Jenny's financial needs and leave the emotional ones to Megan.

"Over my dead body."

"I'm her father," he said, the words sounding as strange as they felt. "One day out of six years isn't a lot to ask for."

"No."

"I can force the issue."

"You wouldn't dare."

"You know damn well there's nothing I wouldn't do."

"Are you threatening me?"

"I don't make threats, Meggie. I get what I want without them."

"She's mine," Megan said, her voice fierce, "and there's nothing you can do to change that."

"One day," he repeated. "Tomorrow. And you can be with her."

"We have plans for tomorrow," Megan said. "I'm

taking Stace and Jenny to the mall for a puppet show. Maybe the day after tomorrow.''

"I'm leaving tomorrow night.''

Her relief was palpable. "Then the next time you're in town.''

"That won't be for at least a year. I'm sailing out of Lahaina next month.''

"For Australia?" she whispered.

He nodded. His dream was finally within reach. He'd expected it to feel a hell of a lot better than it did.

An odd expression flickered across her face but vanished before he could put a name to it. "Jenny has her heart set on the puppet show," Megan said. "She wouldn't understand.''

He thought of his own childhood where disappointment had been the air he breathed. "Then I'll go to the bloody puppet show with you.''

"You'll hate it.''

"You're probably right.''

"She doesn't like you very much.''

"I know," he said grimly. "I don't like her very much, either.''

All in all, they were off to a bloody awful start.

# Chapter Ten

"I think he's cu-uu-ute," said Stace as Megan tried to wrestle her into her pajamas later that evening. Of course she was talking about Jake.

Jenny, already clad in her Little Mermaid nightshirt, turned a somersault on her bed. "I think he's dumb."

Megan fastened the last button on Stace's pajama top. "We don't call people dumb, Jenny."

"He's pretty," Stace cooed dreamily, obviously in the throes of a major crush. "He could be a movie star."

Jenny aimed a withering glance in her friend's direction, then looked at Megan. "Can we have pecan pancakes for breakfast tomorrow?"

"If Ingrid has pecans in the kitchen."

"My mommy always has pecans," Stace declared. "She keeps 'em in the pantry in a big red jar."

"Then it's pecan pancakes tomorrow morning." Megan ruffled Stace's blond curls. "But now it's time for the two of you to go to bed."

"Can't I stay up late tonight?" Jenny asked. "It's my birthday."

"You've had a big day, sweetheart," said Megan, enveloping her daughter in a hug. "I really think you should get some sleep."

Jenny's lower lip quivered. "But it's my birthday."

"I could tell you a story," Megan volunteered. "But only if you two get into bed."

The two little girls scrambled beneath the covers of their respective beds.

"'Cinderella,'" said Jenny. "Just like you told it last night."

"Hooray!" Stace piped up. "Cinderella and the handsome prince from Austria."

Megan didn't bother to correct her. She launched into a rollicking version of "Cinderella" complete with music and sound effects. The girls were enraptured. She followed up "Cinderella" with an abbreviated "Sleeping Beauty," then declared story time officially over for the night.

"You'll see a better version of 'Sleeping Beauty' tomorrow at the mall," she said, giving each little girl a kiss.

"Do you think my mommy will have the baby tonight?" Stace asked as Megan was about to switch off the light.

"Yes, honey, I do. I think by the time you wake up in the morning you'll have a beautiful little brother or sister of your very own."

Miguel had called right around dinnertime to speak to Stace and to let Megan know that Ingrid was heading into the home stretch.

"Aunt Meg." Stace tugged at Megan's sleeve. "Can Jenny have a baby brother?"

Megan looked from Stace to her daughter. "Not right now," she answered. "I'd like to be married before I have another baby."

"You don't have to be married," Jenny piped up.

"I know that, Jenny."

"You could go to the store and get one," Stace chimed in. "My Aunt Lisa did that."

"No, silly," Jenny countered. "Not a store. It's a squirm bank."

"I think it's time we turned out the lights," said Megan, feeling faint. "Now sleep well."

They knew so much—yet they knew nothing at all. And it would be another twenty years before they even realized it.

With a sigh, she headed toward the kitchen to finish cleaning up. The melancholy mood that had begun with Jake's appearance at their daughter's birthday party persisted. Ingrid and Miguel were about to welcome a new member into their family while Megan felt as if she were running in place. Her past, her present and her future had unexpectedly converged and she found herself at the crossroads without a compass.

But not without memories.

*THE NURSE LOOKED UP from the sheaf of papers. "Are you sure you don't want to call someone?" Her expression was kind. "First labor can take a long time. You might like the company."*

*Megan shook her head.* "Thank you, no. I'll be fine."

*The nurse looked dubious.* "There must be someone," *she persisted.* "I know you're not one of our Lamaze patients but still...."

*Megan smiled but remained silent.* I have no one, *she thought as an attendant wheeled her to her hospital room.* There isn't one person on earth I can call to help me.

*For weeks she'd found herself thinking about Jake, dreaming about the man who was her baby's father. Ridiculous, elaborate dreams—fantasies, really— where he would show up on her doorstep and sweep her up into his strong arms and she would be safe and protected.* "I love you, Meggie," *he said in her dreams,* "and I'll love our child more than life itself."

"Fool," *she whispered.*

"Did you say something?" *asked the attendant.*

"No," *said Megan, blinking away sudden tears.*

*Everywhere she looked she saw expectant mothers surrounded by an army of family and friends. Proud husbands, nervous mothers and fathers, friends there to lend support and celebrate a brand-new life. It seemed so little to ask, to have someone with her to share the most important day of her life.*

Jake, *she thought.* Before today is over you'll be a father.

"Do you need help changing into a gown?" *the attendant asked.*

*Megan shook her head.* "I can manage."

*The attendant nodded.* "Someone will be in shortly

*to examine you." The woman disappeared in a flurry
of disinfectant and laundry bleach and that odd smell
that belonged to hospitals alone.*

*From somewhere she heard the sound of laughter
and a soft rush of footsteps past her door. She stiffened
as a contraction came and went, stronger and more
powerful than the one before. She rubbed her belly,
feeling more alone and frightened than she had at any
other time in her life.*

*"I'm going to do right by you," she whispered to
the child eager to be born. "You'll always have me to
rely on."*

THE EXPERIENCE HAD BEEN terrifying and wondrous
and all things in between and Megan would have
given anything for the comfort of having someone
who loved her help her through it. When they'd placed
Jenny in her arms for the first time, she'd been over-
whelmed by a sense of loss so profound that it took
her breath away. Jake should have been there with
them and he would have been if she hadn't been so
eager to run back to the comfort of her father's house.

For all she knew Ingrid was giving birth at this very
moment. Miguel would be there by her side, holding
her hand, calming her fears, there to share the trium-
phant joy of hearing their child's first cry. How would
it feel to share the good times and the bad with someone who would love Jenny as much as Megan did and
be there to protect her if Megan could not?

"A dream," she said aloud, trying to shake off the
persistent mood. She had a healthy, happy child and

that should be enough for any woman. Dreaming about what could have been was an exercise in futility. If she'd learned anything on the *Sea Goddess*, she'd learned that.

*The warmth of his hands against her body...the smell of his skin...the realization that she would never feel so female, so loved if she lived to be one thousand....*

Her thoughts skidded to a halt. Love had nothing to do with what they'd shared. Sensuality, yes. Raw sex, absolutely. But love? Love was for the girl she'd left behind years ago, the one who believed in happy endings and real-life heroes. Love, in its purest form, was what she felt for Jenny. She and Jake wouldn't know love if they fell over it...or into it.

Love was what Miguel and Ingrid felt for each other. That willingness to be there during the bad times and not run away in search of sunnier climes the way she herself had done at the first sign of difficulty. Sometimes it was hard to be around Miguel and Ingrid and not feel a sharp stab of envy that what they had in abundance had been denied to her.

And Jenny felt it too. She'd seen her little girl's face when Jenny came home from Stace's house after Megan's weekend on the *Sea Goddess*. Jenny's talk had been filled with baby brothers and daddies who told bedtime stories and knew how to saddle a horse. Megan's heart had ached at the longing in her little girl's voice. How could she explain to Jenny that sometimes even a daddy could break your heart in two?

*He doesn't want to be your father, sweetheart,* she

thought, resting her head on the smooth surface of the tabletop. If she'd been expecting an argument on that count, Jake had surprised her. Tomorrow he would spend the day with Jenny and tomorrow night he would walk out of their lives for good.

"You should be happy," Megan said in the silent kitchen. "This is exactly what you wanted."

So why was she crying?

IT OCCURRED TO JAKE around midnight that the thing to do was abandon ship. He'd been trying to nap on a couch in the Tropicale office but each time he closed his eyes all he could see was that little red-haired girl barreling toward him like an avenging angel.

*Leave my mommy alone!*

He sat up in the darkened office and dragged a weary hand through his hair. Maybe the little sheila was right. Maybe the best thing he could do was leave them both alone. His rental car was parked downstairs. All he had to do was grab his briefcase and head out to Miami International and board the first plane to Hawaii. This time tomorrow he could be on his boat, alone the way he'd planned it, and today would be just another memory.

*"JAKE." Megan's voice was low, unbearably sexy. "Someone might see us."*

*"We're alone, Meggie. There's no one around for miles."* Just the sea and the stars and the endless night.

*The sailboat rose and fell with the movement of the ocean, urging them closer.*

*"This isn't our boat," she persisted. "What if someone finds out?"*

*"Nobody will find out. We'll be back at the marina before anyone knows it's missing." He'd been desperate to get her out of their tiny, sweltering apartment. Desperate to provide a touch of the luxury she'd known with her father.*

*He moved between her thighs. She moaned as he found her with his hand. "Open for me, Meggie," he said. He needed to lose himself in her softness and heat, feel the way her body tightened around him, hear the sounds she made in the back of her throat when she came.*

*He needed to believe this wasn't the beginning of the end....*

THREE DAYS LATER Megan was gone.

He stared out the office window at the lights of Miami twinkling below. Nothing about that night had been careful or considered. He'd taken her with a fierce hunger that scared them both. She'd responded in kind, drawing him more deeply inside her body until neither one knew where the other began.

Was that the night Jennifer had been conceived? Created out of desire and love and the absolute certainty that what they had together would never be enough to see them through.

He looked at the telephone. One call was all it would take. He could have a plane waiting for him at the airport and be gone before daybreak. There was nothing for him here. Not really. Megan had made it perfectly clear that there was no room for him in her life. And he wasn't convinced there should be room for him in their daughter's. He'd see to it that they never wanted for anything and vanish into his old world.

But dawn found him watching the sunrise over the water.

And at ten o'clock he climbed into his car and started the engine.

Traffic was light as he cut across the city toward the house where Megan was staying. How did she feel spending the night in luxury when her own place was just a step above an army barracks? Did it even matter to her anymore?

Nothing about her life was the way he thought it would be.

He signaled a turn into the subdivision where her partner lived. He should have left well enough alone, kept his memories where they belonged, buried in a far corner of his mind. They were supposed to have great sex, burn away the past, then say goodbye forever. Neat. Clean. Permanent. He hadn't expected to feel as if his soul had been laid bare.

He pulled into the driveway next to a beat-up Ford he now knew to be Megan's. Hard to imagine her without the fiery little red Porsche that had been her trademark.

Hell, he thought, as he headed up the walkway toward the front door. That was just one of a hundred things that had changed in the past six years.

"I have a brand-new baby brother!" The little blond girl with the big blue eyes greeted him as she swung open the door. She was so sweet, so cute, so uncomplicated—everything he'd expected a little girl to be. "His name is Charlie and he weighs ten pounds."

Jake winced. "Ten pounds?"

The little girl nodded, her blond curls bouncing. "My daddy says he's a bowling ball in diapers."

He had to laugh. "I think I'd like your daddy."

"You would like him, Jake." Megan's low voice drifted toward him. "Miguel's a yacht builder."

He looked past Stace to see Megan standing in the archway to the foyer. She wore white pants and a silky pale gold sweater that skimmed her breasts and hips. Her auburn hair was piled loosely on top of her head, anchored with a tortoiseshell pin. She walked toward him, that swaying womanly walk that had always brought him instantly to life.

"Where is she?" he asked.

"In the backyard. She wanted to pick some flowers to take to Ingrid and the baby after the puppet show."

"Won't they wilt?"

"I tried to tell her," Megan said, "but she has her own ideas."

Genetics, he thought. Stubborn genes on both sides of the family. Poor little sheila didn't stand a chance.

It took a good ten minutes to get Jenny and Stace strapped into the back seat of Jake's shiny black Jaguar. They were in a giggly mood, acting about as silly as it was possible for two six-year-old girls to act.

"You have thirty seconds to calm down and get those seat belts fastened," Megan warned. "Otherwise you can forget about the puppet show."

They managed to stop giggling long enough to obey Megan but the laughter started up again as soon as the car was moving.

It was business as usual for Megan. Jake, however, kept glancing at them through the rearview mirror, a puzzled expression on his face.

"This comes with the territory," Megan explained. "Little kids laugh a lot."

He glanced at her and her heart turned over at the surprising look of vulnerability in his eyes. There was something different about him today. Yesterday's anger was gone and in its place was a bittersweet sense of finality that was almost enough to crumble her defenses.

"I think the little ankle-biters are laughing at me."

"They're not laughing at you."

"How do you know?" He glanced in the mirror once again. "I heard the word 'kangaroo.'"

"Oh, Jake!" She started to laugh herself. "That doesn't mean anything."

"I don't know." He didn't sound convinced. "There's something going on back there."

"Of course there's something going on back there. There always is when you're with kids. You'll get used to it."

Her words hung in the air between them. He wasn't going to be around long enough to get used to it. By this time tomorrow he'd be back on another of his yachts, smiling at the pretty women and counting up his profits, while Megan and Jenny went on with their lives as if he'd never existed.

JAKE STARED AT THE SWARM of kids tearing around the center court of the mall. He'd never seen so many children in one place in his life. Hundreds of them, all different ages and colors and personalities, with just one goal in mind: to drive their parents crazy.

Jennifer and Stace had seemed like relatively civilized children to him up until the moment they saw the hordes of small marauders tearing from the carousel to the puppet theater to the child-size railroad that wound its way around the perimeter of the center court.

"Can we sit in the front row, Mommy?" Jennifer's eyes were wide.

"Only if you promise to behave yourselves and not stand up on your chairs."

"We promise," the two children said in unison.

"You believe them?" Jake asked as the girls took their seats right in front of the puppet theater.

Megan shrugged her lovely shoulders. "Hope springs eternal. Ask any mother."

He watched her as she watched their daughter. It occurred to him that the girl he'd loved and lost had been replaced by a woman he would never get to know. Not really. He'd shared her body but would probably never be lucky enough to share her soul and that struck him as a bloody shame.

The puppet show began on schedule and, to Jake's amazement, the kids quieted down enough for the performers to be heard.

"They'll be busy for a while," he said to Megan. "Why don't we get some coffee?"

Megan shook her head. "I can't leave them alone."

"We won't leave the mall."

"No, Jake. You don't understand," she replied, her voice soft. "I have to keep them in my sight at all times."

It was a dangerous world and children were the most vulnerable of them all. The fact that their daughter was a healthy and happy six-year-old was a testament to Megan's devotion and care—and another example of all the things he'd never understand about raising a child.

They sat together on a bench at the side of the puppet stage, opposite the row where Jenny and Stace sat.

"Sometimes I look at Jenny and I wonder how on earth I ever believed I could bring up a child. She's so little, so trusting—" Her voice caught and he put his arm around her shoulders. She didn't move away.

"You're doing a great job with her, Meggie. She's bright and opinionated and—"

She met his eyes. "Stubborn as hell?"

He grinned. "I was saving that for last."

"She's our daughter, Jake. There's no doubt about that."

"Poor kid," Jake sympathized with a laugh.

"Yeah," said Megan softly. "Poor kid."

"She doesn't like me much."

"She doesn't really know you."

"Why don't I think that would help?"

"Maybe she senses how uncomfortable you are around her. Kids are amazingly intuitive."

"It's more than that. When she looks at me I feel like she knows every lousy thing I've done in my life."

Megan chuckled. "She's a brilliant child but you're giving her way too much credit."

"She sees something, Meggie. She knows I don't have what it takes."

"Maybe she sees what you want her to see."

He had no answer for that. He doubted if there was one.

They sat together, his arm around her shoulders, her hand in his, watching the puppet show and enjoying Jenny's reaction to it. Her face was exceptionally mobile, her expressions perfectly mirroring the action on stage. She was bright, enthusiastic, self-confident as hell. He wasn't sure if he was seeing Megan as a child or the kid he would have been if life had dealt him a different hand.

The puppet show concluded after an endless finale of knock-knock jokes and sing-alongs. The minute the curtain went down, the children exploded into frenzied activity, racing for the bathroom, the mini-train and the carousel.

"Can we have a ride, Mommy?" Jennifer begged.

"Please, please, I promise I'll go to sleep on time tonight."

"Please, Aunt Meg," Stace urged. "Just one ride."

"Go ahead, Aunt Meg," Jake said. "I'll pay for it."

Megan looked at the two little girls, then shrugged. "I know when I'm outnumbered."

They bought tickets from a perky little blonde in candy-striped shorts, then waited in line.

"Aunt Meg, help me!" Stace ran for a painted pony the second their turn came. "I can't climb up."

Megan hesitated.

"Go ahead," Jake said, sounding more confident than he felt. "I'll help Jennifer."

Jennifer looked up at him and scowled. "I don't want you," she declared, standing in front of a palomino with pink flowers painted around his neck. "I want my mommy to help me."

"Sorry, kid," he replied, stung. "Looks like you're stuck with me."

Her lower lip jutted forward ominously.

"Hey, none of that." He grabbed her by the waist. She was so tiny, her bones so small and delicate—

"Not that way!" She wriggled out of his grasp, giggling. He'd never heard a sound quite like that before. Not in the house where he grew up. "That tickles."

"What tickles?" he asked, taking her by the waist again. "This?"

Her giggles grew louder. "You're doing it wrong!"

He let her slip out of his grasp again. Her golden eyes twinkled with merriment.

"So how do I do it right?"

"Here," she said, pointing under her arms. "That's how my mommy does it."

"How do you know your mommy does it the right way?"

"Because my mommy knows how to do everything."

A lump the size of Gibraltar formed in his throat and he swallowed hard, trying to dislodge it. Out of all their fire and all the pain, he and Megan had created this perfect little girl.

He put his hands under her arms and swung her up onto the painted palomino. "Your mommy is a very good mommy, isn't she?"

Her eyes were on a level with his. "My mommy is the best in the world." She peered at him curiously. "Your eyes are wet."

"No, they're not."

She leaned forward and touched his cheek with the tip of her finger. "Yes, they are."

"I have a cold."

"You haven't sneezed once."

"I have a sneezeless cold."

She giggled again. "You're silly."

"Yeah," he agreed, smiling at her. "Sometimes I am."

The carousel lurched forward and he made to jump off.

"No!" Jenny grabbed for his shoulder. "You have to stay, too. I'm just a kid. I could fall off."

"We wouldn't want that to happen." He glanced around, surprised to see that for every young rider there was an adult.

"You have to stand real close," Jenny ordered. "Mommy always holds the horse's leash."

"Reins," he said. "The horse's reins."

A big dimple appeared in her left cheek. *Oh, God,* he thought. *My mother had a dimple in her left cheek.* He hadn't really thought about his mother in years and now he could see her standing in front of him.

"You didn't laugh," she said, brows slanting into a frown. "I told a joke."

"Sorry, Jennifer. I was thinking of something else." He focused his attention on her. "Tell me your joke again."

"Horses don't have reins," she said, "clouds have rains."

He stared at her, dumbstruck.

"You're not laughing," she said, looking disappointed. "Don't you get it?"

"I get it," he said, as a laugh, a real one, erupted. The kid understood homonyms. His chest felt swollen with something suspiciously like pride.

"Really?" asked Jennifer, her eyes sparkling with pride.

"Really," he said, patting her awkwardly on the head.

He couldn't bring himself to look over at Megan. He felt naked, his emotions exposed. It was like a different man had crawled inside his skin, a man who wanted things he couldn't have. Things he wouldn't know how to handle if he did have them.

"Why do you call me Jennifer?" she asked as the carousel slowed down.

"That's your name, isn't it?"

"Only teachers call me Jennifer." She made a funny face. "You should call me Jenny."

"Jenny." He swung her from the horse, aware of the way her hair smelled of shampoo, of the delicate framework of bone and muscle, of how she was everything good and right about the time he and Megan had spent together.

"Do you have a little girl of your own?"

"Uh…" He hesitated. Talk about a loaded question. "Yeah," he said after a long moment. "I do."

"I don't have a daddy," she confided. "He and my mommy got di—" she paused, searching for the right word "—divorced a long time ago. We haven't seen him since I was in mommy's tummy."

"Your mom does a good job taking care of you, doesn't she?"

Jenny nodded vigorously. "But I still wish I had a daddy. Daddies take you lots of places." She looked at him. "Besides, Mommy says she won't have a new baby unless we have a daddy."

There was no safe response to that one so he just let her comment pass.

He started toward the ticket booth where Megan and Stace were waiting.

"You have to hold my hand," Jenny said, looking

up at him. "Don't you hold your little girl's hand? Kids can get lost in malls."

"We wouldn't want that to happen, would we?"

Her hand disappeared within his. A feeling of such tenderness, such painful towering joy washed over him that for a second he couldn't draw a breath. He had to remind himself that it was only for one day.

"ARE YOU CRYING, Aunt Meg?" Stace tugged at her hand. "Why are you crying?"

"I'm not crying, Stace." Megan blinked quickly, wishing little girls didn't have such sharp eyes. "It's my allergies."

"You were crying," Stace persisted, very much the forthright Ingrid's daughter. "I saw you."

*Oh, Stace, you'd cry too if you were watching a miracle unfold right before your eyes.*

The look on Jake's face was unmistakable. Something had happened on that carousel, some wondrous incredible event that had cracked open his heart and let his daughter creep inside. Jenny was holding Jake's hand and talking animatedly while Jake leaned toward her, listening intently.

They looked so perfect together. Right down to the way she tilted her head, Jenny was her father's daughter. People used to comment on the resemblance between Megan and her own father. Megan would beam with pride each time her handsome father pulled out the chair for her in a fancy restaurant and ordered up a Shirley Temple "on the rocks."

Despite everything there were still many happy

memories and she wondered if it was fair to deny Jenny the chance to know her own father.

"I rode the palomino, Mommy." Jenny's face was aglow. "And Jake held the lea—" She stopped and looked up at Jake. "What was that again?"

"Remember your joke," he prodded. "The one about clouds…?"

"The reins!"

"Way to go, Jenny."

*Jenny.* Megan's heart flipped over inside her chest at the sound of their daughter's name on his lips. She was foolish to feel this way and she knew it. She and Jenny were doing fine on their own. They didn't need any complications.

"Aunt Meg." Stace tugged at her hand. "You said we could go see Mommy and my brother now."

Jake met her eyes. "What about lunch?"

"Stace can't wait any longer. I figured we would stop by the hospital for a visit, then go on to lunch from there."

"Aw, Mommy, do we have to?" Jenny looked disgruntled.

"I thought you wanted to give Aunt Ingrid the flowers."

"*After* lunch," Jenny protested, "not *before.*"

"But you said we could, Aunt Meg!" Stace's big blue eyes welled with tears. "I want to see Charlie."

"Charlie's a dumb name for a baby," said Jenny. "I don't want to go."

"You're dumb!" said Stace.

"You are!"

"One more word, Jenny, and you're going home."
It was just a kids' squabble but Megan was embarrassed that it was happening in front of Jake.

"I don't care," Jenny said, lower lip jutting forward. "I—"

Megan watched in amazement as Jake bent down and said something to Jenny in a quiet voice. Jenny's ears reddened and she shook her head. Jake said something more, then Jenny nodded. "I'm sorry," Jenny mumbled. "I want to see the baby, too."

Stace thought about it for a few seconds then smiled. "Okay."

They all started for the parking lot, the two little girls holding hands and walking a few feet ahead of Megan and Jake.

"I won't even ask what you said to her. A wise woman never questions magic."

"A little Aussie charm goes a long way."

"Apparently so."

"She's a smart kid. She didn't want to hurt Stace. She's just put out because Stace has a new brother."

Megan started to laugh. "And if her mother had told her that she would have thrown a tantrum right there in the middle of the mall. Children always seem to listen to strangers—"

CONVERSATION STOPPED cold. If Megan had been looking for a way to bring him back to reality, she'd found it with one sentence.

A stranger, he thought as he drove toward the hospital.

His blood ran through Jenny's veins and it didn't matter a damn in the scheme of things. He hadn't seen Megan's belly grow large with their child or felt the child move beneath his hand. He hadn't been there for Jenny's birth, heard her first cry, watched her take her first step. All of the sentimental milestones that marked a family's life and he hadn't been there for a one of them.

When Megan had walked out on him she'd changed the course of three lives forever.

One day wasn't going to make a difference.

He'd walk away with a handful of memories and by this time tomorrow Jenny wouldn't remember he existed.

# Chapter Eleven

"I must say you look disgustingly beautiful for a woman who gave birth less than twelve hours ago." Megan embraced her partner. "You give the pain of childbirth a bad name."

"You should have seen me a few hours ago." Ingrid laughed. "It was not a pretty sight."

In truth Ingrid never looked anything but splendid. And, Megan noted, never more lovely than she did right now with her newborn son cradled against her breast.

"Oh, Ingrid—" Megan's breath caught as she touched the infant's downy cheek "—he's wonderful."

"And hungry," Ingrid said. "I have a feeling this one is going to end up playing for the Dolphins in a few years."

"Stace is beside herself with excitement," Megan said. "All she could talk about was Charlie."

Jenny and Stace had already visited Ingrid and the baby. Jenny's handpicked flowers occupied a place of honor next to a splashy bouquet from Miguel's parents. A nurse had taken the girls for a trip to the nursery to look at the pair of twins who'd been born right after Charlie.

"So where is he?" Ingrid asked, moving Charlie to her left breast.

"In the waiting room. He didn't feel right coming in to see you."

"I'm disappointed. I wanted to meet him."

"That's probably one of the reasons he's in the waiting room."

"Don't tell me that gorgeous hunk of man is shy?"

"Who said he's a gorgeous hunk of man?" Megan countered.

"Stace couldn't stop talking about him," she said, kissing Charlie atop his head. "You lied, Meg. Her baby brother ran a poor second."

"I'm afraid Stace has a major crush on Jake." She sighed. "Jenny's not too crazy about him, though."

"That's not what she said to me." Ingrid met Megan's eyes. "She said he'd be a perfect daddy."

"That's not funny, Ingrid."

"It isn't meant to be. Jenny said that he told her he has a little girl of his own."

"Oh God...." Megan buried her face in her hands. "I've made a hash of things, Ingrid. A week ago everything made sense, but now...."

"You're in love with him. It isn't a crime."

"I'm not in love with him."

"Right," said Ingrid, glancing down at her chest. "And I'm not breast-feeding." She paused a moment.

"When are you going to tell Jenny that he's her father?"

Megan peered at Ingrid from between her fingers. "We're not."

"You're making a mistake, Megan. A big one."

"Telling her would be a mistake. Jake has no intention of staying around to be part of her life. In fact he's leaving tonight for God knows where. Why complicate things for Jenny?"

"It seems to me they're complicated enough already."

"Back off, Ingrid. I think I know what's best for Jenny."

Ingrid stared her down. "And I think I know what's best for you. You're a lousy liar, Megan. Sooner or later you'll have to tell Jenny. Don't make it any more complicated than it already is."

"Thanks for the advice, Dr. Chavez. I'll keep it in mind."

"Being in love isn't a crime."

Megan glared at her friend. "If you weren't breast-feeding, I'd tell you to put up your dukes."

"Face it, Megan, you never got over him. It's Jake Lockwood and it always will be."

"That's a lousy thing to say."

"Like it or not, the three of you are a family. Why not give things a chance? Put all of your cards on the table and let fate decide." Ingrid waited. A broad smile spread across her face. "What's wrong, Megan? No answer for that one?"

"I have an answer," Megan said, "and when I think of it I'll let you know."

JAKE WAS FLIPPING through a copy of *American Baby* when Jenny raced into the waiting room then skidded to a halt in front of him. "I saw twins in the baskets! One has red hair and the other's bald!" She grabbed his hand and tugged. "Don't you want to see them?"

"Haven't given it much thought, Jenny." Staring at babies under glass had never been high on his list.

"You have to see them."

"Did you see Charlie yet?"

"He's cute," Jenny said, "but the twins are cuter."

He glanced around. "Where's Stace?" The two of them were rarely apart.

"She went home with her Aunt Carmen." She tugged at his hand again. "Come *on!*"

Jenny dragged him down the hall to the nursery where Jake looked through the glass at a smorgasbord of babies on display.

"Those snorkers are little," he said, staring at the sea of tiny faces. "I thought they'd be bigger than that."

Next to him Jenny giggled. "What's a snorker?"

He ruffled her hair. "You were a snorker when you were their age."

"Is that what they call babies in Australia?"

"That's one of the things." He looked down at his daughter. "Wonder what you looked like when you were a snorker?"

"I was bald," Jenny informed him proudly.

"Mommy told me that she was afraid I'd be bald forever."

*You missed it, mate, and there's no way you can ever get it back.*

"Your mommy must have been relieved when all of your pretty red hair began to come in."

Jenny nodded vigorously. "She took pictures of me every single day."

*She's your daughter, Lockwood, but you'll never be part of her life.*

He nodded toward an older woman who'd joined them at the window.

"Charlie's crying!" Jenny pointed toward the baby the nurse had just placed in the third isolette from the left.

Jake looked at the squalling infant. "How do you know that's Charlie?"

"Because it is," said Jenny. "I just know."

The woman next to him touched his arm. "Their names are posted on the foot of the isolettes."

Jenny straightened up to full height. "I can't read yet," she announced. "I know it's Charlie because he looks like Aunt Ingrid."

The woman looked from Jenny to Jake. "Just like you two. She's the spitting image of her daddy. Same beautiful gold eyes."

"He's not my daddy," Jenny said.

"Oh, come now," the woman persisted. "You're two peas in a pod."

Jake cleared his throat. "She looks just like her mother." Lame, but it was the best he could do on short notice. He turned to Jenny. "Why don't you go tell your Aunt Ingrid that Charlie's hungry. I'll meet you here in five minutes and we'll get burritos."

Jenny was gone in a flash of auburn hair.

"Your little girl certainly has been blessed in the looks department," the woman said then stopped. "But she isn't your little girl, is she?"

"No," he said. The lie tore at his gut but he couldn't risk being overheard by Jenny. "She's not my little girl."

He looked up to see Megan striding toward him.

"Where's Jenny?" she asked without preamble.

"Off to talk to Ingrid. Are you ready for lunch?"

Megan shot him a look of pure disgust, then wheeled and disappeared down the hallway.

"Quite a temper," said the woman. "I hope her little girl didn't inherit it."

"Lady," said Jake, "why don't you shut up?"

SHE'S NOT MY LITTLE GIRL.

His words were a knife in her heart.

If Megan had entertained any fantasies of a happy ending for the three of them, Jake's comment to the curious woman at the nursery window brought them to a screeching halt.

Jenny meant no more to him than Stace did. She was just another cute little girl with dimples who happened to find him as charming as he liked to think he was. You couldn't trust him. You couldn't depend on him. At the first sign of trouble he'd be so busy covering his own behind that he'd forget she and Jenny even existed.

He was no better than her father had been and she'd been the worst kind of fool for falling for his line when she should have known better.

She heard his footsteps behind her but she didn't turn around.

He caught up with her a few yards away from the nursery.

"What the hell's wrong with you?" he asked, grabbing her by the arm.

She pulled out of his grasp. "Nothing's wrong."

"Don't lie to me, Meggie."

"Don't call me Meggie. Don't ask me what's wrong. This whole thing has been ridiculous and I'm putting an end to it now."

"Don't I have any say in it?"

"No," she said fiercely. "You don't have any say in it at all. I'm taking Jenny and we're going home."

"The hell you are."

"The hell I'm not. I heard you back there, Jake. You don't care about her. Why don't you just let her go before she becomes any more attached to you than she already is?"

"She's not attached to me. By tomorrow morning she'll forget I existed."

"Wishful thinking," she shot back, "or do you really know so little about human nature?"

"I know children. They're resilient. Right now all I am is a man with a strange accent who told a few kangaroo stories and made her laugh."

"And that's enough for you."

"You say it as if you're disappointed."

"I'm not disappointed," she snapped. "This is what we agreed on. One day and you're out of her life."

"The day's not over yet."

She turned on her heel and stormed back toward the nursery. This time he didn't follow her. She could feel his eyes hot on her back but she didn't slow her pace or turn around. She didn't want him tangling up Jenny's life the way he'd tangled up hers but she hated the fact that he was willing to give up their daughter without a fight.

How could he not see how special she was? How miraculous? Didn't he want to know what she'd been like as a baby? Wasn't he even the slightest bit curious to know about the chain of birthdays and Christmases and everyday living that had produced the little girl he knew as his daughter?

Once again she'd allowed her idiotic fantasies to get the better of her common sense. Fathers were made not born. The mysteries of genetics and bloodlines weren't enough to turn a man into a father.

And Jake was proof of that.

He didn't deserve Jenny, and Megan was going to put an end to this charade before it went any further.

Jenny was waiting by the elevators near the nursery.

"Honey." Megan's voice was shaky, unnaturally high. She took a deep breath. "Come on, Jen. It's time to go."

"Good," Jenny responded with a big smile. "I'm hungry."

Megan pushed the down button.

"Where's Jake?" Jenny asked. "Can't he come with us, Mommy?"

"Not this time, honey. Jake has something else to do."

"But he said."

"Sometimes grown-ups can't do everything they say they will."

"That's not fair."

She stroked Jenny's hair. "I know, honey."

Everything about this was unfair, Megan thought as they rode down to the lobby. Whatever happened to happy endings? If this was a movie instead of real life she and Jenny would never have made it to the elevator before Jake came running after them, pledging his love and devotion.

"I want Jake to come with us," Jenny said.

"He has other things to do, Jen."

"Doesn't he like you?"

"I don't know, honey."

"He has to like you. He's our friend." That stubborn little lower lip jutted forward. "You said so."

"You didn't seem to like him very much yesterday," Megan pointed out. "You weren't very nice."

"He didn't like me," Jenny said, "but now he does."

That awful lump was back in Megan's throat. "How do you know?"

"I just do, that's all."

They rode down the rest of the way in silence.

JAKE WATCHED THEM STEP into the elevator as a feeling of emptiness settled inside his chest. Everything had gone wrong so quickly that he had the sense of standing in the aftermath of a tornado. He didn't notice the beautiful woman in a crimson silk dressing gown as she walked slowly toward him.

"You have to be Jake," she said, offering her hand. "Stace described you perfectly."

He looked down at her, bringing himself back to reality. "And you have to be Ingrid."

She nodded. "Where's Megan?" she asked, looking around.

"She left."

Ingrid's lips pursed. "She likes to do that."

"I've noticed."

"We had a loud…disagreement."

Jake met her eyes. "So did we."

"Stubborn, isn't she?"

"She has reason."

Ingrid took a good long look at him. "You're gorgeous but you're not too bright, are you? The girl is still in love with you, Jake. She's never stopped being in love with you."

"She hates my guts." A woman in love didn't look at a man as if he were a failure at the things that counted.

"I don't like my husband all the time, but that doesn't mean I don't love him."

"Nobody's talking about love. We're talking about Jenny. She deserves a stable family. A real home."

All the things that he'd never known, the things he'd said didn't matter.

Ingrid sighed. "I've never seen two people so willing to walk away from happiness in my life. Who said it had to be easy, Jake? Who said you wouldn't have to work hard to make it last?"

"You don't experiment with a child's life." He glared at Ingrid. "You have two kids. You should understand."

"You know," said Ingrid after a moment, "maybe you're right. It takes guts to build a family. Maybe you and Megan just don't have what it takes after all."

Her words followed him into the elevator. They taunted him all the way down to the lobby. She thought he was a coward. A quitter. She never used the words but her meaning had been clear.

He'd never been a coward or a quitter in his life and yet he'd approached his own daughter with an uncertainty and caution that ran counter to everything he was. Everything he'd believed himself to be.

So what if his own father had been a failure at the game? That didn't mean Jake was cursed to follow suit.

And who gave a damn if Darrin McLean had cared more for himself than for his daughter? That was ancient history. She deserved better than that and Jake was the one who could give it to her, even if she went to the altar kicking and screaming.

Damn it, he thought, as he headed for the hospital exit. Ingrid was right. They'd been given a second chance and they were about to toss it aside like yesterday's newspaper. He and Megan and Jenny were a family and it was time they started acting like one.

He headed toward the parking lot. *It's not over yet for us, Meggie. We're going to make this work...for us and for Jenny.* It was time he took matters into his own hands.

"WE DON'T HAVE A CAR," Jenny pointed out as she and Megan stood on the sidewalk in front of the hospital. "How are we going to get home?"

"There's a taxi stand across the street," Megan said. So what if they had to eat spaghetti for the next month. The important thing was to put as much distance between her and Jake as she possibly could.

*She's not my little girl....* His words echoed in her brain again and again. *She's not my little girl....*

*It's what you wanted, isn't it?* that small voice inside her taunted. *You want her all to yourself. No father to share her with.*

For six years it had seemed so clear-cut, so right, that she'd never questioned her position. Now the questions she'd tried so hard to avoid were crowding in on her, pushing against her heart, forcing her to acknowledge that the choices she'd made might no longer be the right ones.

Not for her.

And especially not for Jenny.

Tears welled in her eyes. *Damn you, Jake Lockwood,* she thought.

"Mommy!" Jenny tugged at her hand. "You're walking too fast."

She stopped on the curb and glanced up and down the street. She could hardly see through the tears threatening to spill down her cheeks. "Sorry, honey."

"Why are you in such a rush?"

"Aren't you hungry for lunch?" she asked with forced cheer. Jenny shouldn't see her like this. "I want to get us a cab and get home."

"But you said we can have burritos for lunch."

They stepped off the curb. "I'll make you burritos at home."

"Yours aren't as good as the ones at Pepito's."

"Thanks a lot," Megan replied as they reached the middle of the street. "Maybe we can—"

The screech of brakes seemed to come from no-where as the truck rounded the corner of the parking lot and barreled straight toward them.

JAKE DIDN'T KNOW what made him turn around. The whine of the auto's engine. Jenny's scream. The bone-deep knowledge that everything he loved, everything that mattered was about to be taken away from him.

He saw the truck bearing down on them. He saw the desperation on Megan's face, the terror on Jenny's.

"Move!" he screamed as he vaulted over a parked car and ran toward them. "Move!"

But they were frozen in place by fear.

Faster...he had to run faster...his lungs burned... adrenaline...he needed that one last burst of adrenaline to push him over the edge....

The truck was a few yards away from them. He

could smell the exhaust. A handful of seconds was all he had left.

With a cry that seemed to come from the depths of his soul he hurtled toward them and prayed it wasn't too late.

## Chapter Twelve

"Never saw anything like it," said a man who'd watched the whole thing happen. "He threw himself right in front of that truck and saved their lives. Guy's a hero, if you ask me."

The policeman nodded, writing down the information in an official-looking pad. "Driver was under the influence," he said with a shake of his head. "Never saw the woman and her little girl."

"Most amazing thing I ever saw," the witness went on. "Not too many heroes in this world. Wish I could shake that guy's hand and tell him so."

*A hero,* Megan thought numbly as she stood in the hallway and watched the emergency-room doctors working on Jake. For as long as she could remember she'd been looking for a hero and he'd been there right under her nose all the time.

"Mommy, what's going to happen to him?" Jenny, blessedly unscratched, stood next to Megan, her golden eyes wide with fright. "Will he die?"

"He wouldn't dare." Megan fought back her tears. "Not now."

"He jumped right in front of the truck, Mommy, like he wasn't afraid of anything in the whole world."

"I know," Megan whispered. "And he did it for us."

"Ma'am." A doctor appeared at her side. "We'd really like to take a look at that bump on your head."

Megan brushed him away. "I'm fine. Worry about Jake."

"You're going to have one nasty bruise." The doctor observed her more closely. "And a black eye if I don't miss my guess."

"Later," she said. "I'll worry about it later." She didn't care if she had two black eyes. Nothing mattered. All she could do was watch as the doctors mumbled over Jake's still body in the next room, whispering things she didn't want to understand.

"Mommy, I want to stay with you." Jenny's eyes seemed too large in her pale face.

"I know you do, honey, but I think you should go visit with Aunt Ingrid for a while."

"But I just saw Aunt Ingrid before."

"Maybe you could watch Charlie nurse."

"What if Jake wakes up and wants to see me?"

"If he does I'll come and get you."

"Really?"

"You have my word."

Miguel showed up a few minutes later to take Jenny upstairs.

"How is he?" Miguel asked quietly, so Jenny wouldn't hear.

Megan shook her head. "I don't know."

"We're praying for him, Meg. For both of you."

She blinked back tears. "Thanks, Miguel, but Jake needs those prayers more than I do."

Miguel took Jenny's hand and they disappeared down the corridor toward the elevator bank. She was so little, so innocent. So sure that life would hand her nothing but roses.

Megan closed her eyes against the image of Jake lying motionless in the street...of Jenny standing next to him, crying as if her heart would break.

So many mistakes. Such a terrible misuse of time. Her mind leapfrogged wildly over the missed opportunities and each one was a knife in the heart. They belonged together, the three of them, and now all she could do was pray they'd have the chance. They could have lived these past six years as a family, building memories that would warm them against the cold winds of fate.

If only she hadn't walked out on him at the first sign of trouble.

If only he hadn't been living in La Mirada when she tried to find him.

If only they'd told each other the truth the first night on the *Sea Goddess*—

The list of "if only's" was endless and it didn't change a thing.

When you came down to it, all you had was the moment. This brief fleeting instant in time that was gone before you drew your next breath.

All she wanted was another chance. One more opportunity to tell him what was in her heart, what had been in her heart from that very first moment when she saw him on the beach in Key West and fell in love.

She paced the length of the waiting room, unmindful of the cut on her knee or the bruises that were blossoming on her hip. She had to keep moving. If she kept moving she'd be able to stay one step ahead of the fear building inside her. She willed her strength into his body, willed her love into his heart.

A lifetime seemed to pass by the time the doctors left Jake's side and approached her.

"Mrs. Lockwood?"

She nodded. This was hardly the time to get technical. "H-how is he?"

The doctor, a slim black woman, sighed. "I wish I could say with some certainty but I can't."

"You can't! What do you mean you can't? You're a doctor, aren't you? You have to know what's—"

The doctor placed a hand on Megan's forearm. "He's unconscious. His vital signs are strong. We've found nothing wrong beyond some broken ribs and a compound fracture of the right leg."

"But he's unconscious. Why is he still unconscious?"

"He sustained a trauma, Mrs. Lockwood. Determining the extent of the trauma takes time. It may be nothing more than a simple concussion. We're going to take him up for an MRI. We'll know a great deal more after that."

"I have to see him," she insisted. "I want to talk to him." *There's something I have to tell him...something I should have told him a long time ago....*

The doctor sighed. "As you wish. But please don't expect a response."

The doctor led her into the room.

"He looks like he's sleeping," Megan said, choking back her tears.

"I can only give you a minute with him, Mrs. Lockwood. They're waiting upstairs to run the MRI."

Megan placed her hand against Jake's cheek. She smiled at the faint scratch of his beard against her palm. Bending down she kissed his forehead. His skin was warm against her lips and a crazy feeling of hope grabbed hold of her and wouldn't let go.

"You'll do anything for attention, won't you, Jake Lockwood? Throwing yourself in front of a moving vehicle like you're some Aussie superman." She forced a laugh. "Can't you find a better way to get the women to notice you?"

Nothing. No response at all.

Was it over? Was it possible that she'd never have the chance to tell him how she felt?

Next to Megan the doctor cleared her throat. "I'm sorry, but the orderlies are here to take Mr. Lockwood up to X-ray."

"One more minute," she begged, unable to tear her eyes away from him. "Please."

The doctor stepped aside again.

Megan placed her lips against Jake's ear. "I love you," she whispered, putting her heart and soul into those simple words. Praying for their healing power to work their magic one more time. "I've never stopped loving you, not for a second. And I know Jenny will love you just as much when I tell her—"

"Wh-when?"

She looked up at the doctor. "Did you hear that?"

The doctor nodded. The expression in her eyes was unmistakable. "Say something more to him."

"Jenny thinks you're a hero, Jake. When I tell her you're her father, she'll—"

"When *we* t-tell her...."

Her breath caught as his eyelids twitched then slowly opened. "Oh, God, Jake! You heard me!"

"M-more than that...you said s-something else...."

She couldn't help it. She threw back her head and she started to laugh. "I love you, Jake Lockwood! I love you, I love you, I love you!"

He motioned for her to move closer, then closer still. "I love you, Meggie...."

She'd heard the words before but somehow they had never sounded as sweet as they did at that moment.

"Shh," she said, kissing him on the mouth. "You don't have to say it. You showed me." Many men talked of love but few understood its deepest meaning. Jake had put his own life on the line so that she and Jenny could live. If there was a better way to say "I love you," she couldn't imagine what it was.

"Jenny...is she—"

"She's fine," Megan managed through her tears as the attendants came to take him to X-ray. "Thanks to you."

"T-tell her," he said, his eyes closing. "Tell her...."

"We'll tell her together," Megan called after him, as the attendants wheeled him from the room.

The two of them.

The way it should be.

THE MRI SHOWED nothing beyond the broken ribs and fractured leg.

"He's a fortunate man," the doctor told Megan the next afternoon. "Must've been born under a lucky star."

Jenny tugged at Megan's hand. "Does that mean Jake was born outside?"

Megan and the doctor laughed.

"No, honey," Megan explained. "That means God was watching over Jake." She turned to the doctor. "It's okay if we go in to see him now?"

"Absolutely. He's not terribly happy with his leg in traction. He could use some company."

"Jake's my friend," Jenny declared, clutching a bouquet of flowers in one hand and her stuffed kangaroo in the other. "He said he wants me to visit him."

"I'm sure he does." The doctor patted Jenny on the head. "You can go in whenever you like."

Now that the moment was finally here, Megan's hands began to tremble. There was no telling how Jenny would react when they broke the news to her. Children never quite behaved the way you thought they should—or even in the way you expected.

She bent down to fix the collar of Jenny's splashy yellow dress. "Remember what I told you about broken legs?"

Jenny nodded solemnly. "Jake's leg is in a swing and I can't play with it."

"That's right." She touched her daughter's cheek. "All of those contraptions might look a little scary, Jenny, but it's all part of what will make Jake get well faster."

"Can we go see him now?"

Megan swallowed hard. "Yes," she said, squaring her shoulders. "I guess this is as good a time as any."

"Jake!" Jenny exploded into the room like a cannonball.

Megan's heart turned over inside her chest. Jake looked like a displaced grizzly bear. There was something about the sight of a big, exceptionally masculine man in a hospital bed that brought out all of her tender feelings. His hair was tousled. His face was stubbled. His bare chest was wrapped in white bandages to bind his ribs. His leg was suspended from a contraption straight out of Rube Goldberg's dreams.

He'd never looked more wonderful.

"Wow!" Jenny stared up at the shiny gear suspended from the ceiling. "Does it hurt?"

Jake winked at Megan. "Only when I laugh."

"Is that a joke?"

"You're a smart little sheila, I'll give you that."

"Sheila?" Jenny's brows drew together in a frown. "I know a girl named Sheila."

Megan put her arm around Jenny's shoulders. "Sometimes they call girls sheilas in Australia."

"Oh," said Jenny. "That's silly."

Megan bent down and whispered in her daughter's ear. "Don't you have something for Jake?"

Jenny nodded. "We brought you flowers," she said, handing them to Jake. "I picked them myself."

Jake grinned. "From Ingrid's backyard?"

Megan shot him a look. "From our own backyard. It's not as impressive as Ingrid's but our flowers are just as terrific."

He took the bouquet and laid it on the bed next to him. "This is great, Jen. Maybe your mom will put them in water for me."

"Don't get used to this, Lockwood," she muttered as she searched the closet for a vase. "Once that leg is mended...."

His laughter warmed her in a way not even the Florida sun could match.

"That's a great kangaroo," Jake said, gesturing toward the stuffed toy in Jenny's arms. "Is that the one you told me about?"

Jenny nodded. "Her name is Sidney." She pushed it toward Jake. "She can be your friend in the hospital."

"You'd let me keep your favorite toy?"

Her expression was solemn. "You'd have to be real careful."

"I would be."

She pointed toward the kangaroo's midsection. "There's something in her pouch."

Megan watched as he fished around in the felt-lined pouch then withdrew her four-leaf clover pendant. He looked up at Megan.

"You were wearing this on the ship."

"Jenny gave it to me for good luck. We both want you to hang on to it until you're on your feet again."

He started to say something but his voice caught and he coughed to cover up. Strong, independent Jake Lockwood brought to his knees by the power of love.

"Is he crying, Mommy?" Jenny asked. "Do you think his leg hurts?"

Megan was finding it hard to speak herself. "C-come here, honey." She sat on the chair next to Jake's bed. "Sit on my lap, okay?"

"I'm not a baby," Jenny said. "Only babies sit on their mother's lap."

"Just this once?" Megan asked. "For me?"

With a terribly grown-up sigh, Jenny gave in and sat on Megan's lap.

Jake was inspecting the kangaroo with great deliberation. "Sidney's pretty cute," he told Jenny.

"I know. Kangaroos are cool."

"Real kangaroos are even better."

"I never saw a real kangaroo."

He glanced over at Megan. "Never?"

Megan shook her head. Her heart was pounding so loudly she could barely hear a word they were saying.

He looked back at Jenny. "How would you like to see a real kangaroo?"

"Where?" asked Jenny. "At the zoo?"

"Not the zoo," he said. "In Australia."

Jenny leaned closer to Megan. "My mommy won't let me go far away without her."

Megan whispered a silent prayer. "What if I came along with you, honey?"

Jenny's eyes widened. "You and me and Jake?"

"Your mom and I are going to get married," Jake said, "as soon as my leg is mended, and then we're going to take you with us to Australia on our honeymoon."

"Does that sound like fun to you?" Megan asked.

The little girl nodded. "Could Stace come, too?"

Megan smiled. "I think Stace should stay with her family, don't you?"

Jenny thought about that for a moment. "I guess." She looked at Jake, then at Megan. "Would we be a family if we went to Australia?"

Jake chuckled but Megan could see he was still as apprehensive as she was. "It takes a little more than going to Australia to make a family. We need a wedding first."

Megan reached for Jake's hand. "Remember how I told you that your daddy and I got divorced before you were born?"

"When I was still in your tummy."

"That's right. Honey, Jake is your daddy."

The child looked at Jake with eyes filled with wonder. "Really?"

He nodded. "Really."

"Where have you been?"

"Everywhere and nowhere," Jake answered, meeting Megan's eyes. "Believe me, if I'd known you were here, Jenny, there's nothing that could have kept me away.''

Megan didn't even try to stem the flow of tears. ''We were lost for a long time, honey, but now that we've found each other nothing will keep us apart. When we get married this time, it will be for ever and ever.''

Jenny looked at her father. ''Are you Jake or are you Daddy?''

''Daddy. Definitely Daddy.''

Jenny's smile could have lit up the city. ''When we go to Australia can I have a kangaroo?''

Jake started to laugh. ''We'll have to ask the kangaroos what they think about that, Jen.''

''Kangaroos can't talk,'' said Jenny, easing onto the bed next to her father. ''Mrs. Daniels at school says...''

It was a simple enough scene. A father and his daughter sitting together, talking about kangaroos and koala bears and kindergarten teachers.

To Megan it was the most beautiful sight on earth. The little girl she loved more than life itself and the man she'd loved and almost lost.

He was the hero of her deepest dreams, the lover of her wildest fantasies, the father of her child and before too long he'd be her husband.

And this time it would be for ever.

# Epilogue

*Two months later*

Jake met her eyes in the mirror. "What do you think?"

"Not that one," Jenny said. "The other one."

He held the tie up to his collar. "Are you sure?"

She nodded vigorously. "That's the one."

He'd never been very good at tying bow ties but this time he got it right on the first shot.

"Does your leg still hurt?"

"I don't think I'll notice it today." He turned around to face her. "So how do I look?"

She made a show of looking him over. "Just right."

He held out his hand. "Time to hit the road."

"Okay, Daddy." She put her hand in his and his heart nearly burst from his chest. He doubted he'd ever get used to the wonder of it all. She looked so grown-up in her fancy dress and earrings. Only six years old yet he could see her mother's grace in every gesture she made.

The transition from stranger to father had been so easy that sometimes he wondered how it was he'd been born beneath such a lucky star.

Jenny tugged at his hand. "Come on, Daddy! Mommy's waiting for us in the living room."

"Just a minute, Jen." He bent down and enveloped her in his arms.

"Daddy, my dress is getting squooshed."

"I love you, Jen."

"Me, too, Daddy."

Even now, two months later, he couldn't quite believe it. This beautiful and independent little girl loved him. She was still a handful, too smart and too precocious for her own good, but the love was there and the trust and he knew that with those two items on his side, everything would be all right.

"It took you long enough." Megan was waiting near the window. She looked like an angel in her ivory dress and upswept hair. "I was beginning to wonder if you two developed cold feet."

Jenny giggled. "It's hot today, Mommy! How can you get cold feet?"

Megan's eyes met his from across the room. He swore he could see the ties that bound them together shimmering in the morning sunlight.

"How are you feeling?" he asked. A simple question but the most important one he'd asked in his life.

"Positively wonderful." Her face was aglow with happiness.

He felt a crazy smile tugging at his mouth. "Positive?"

She nodded. "Positive. Think that fancy sailboat of yours can handle all of us?"

He swept her into his arms and started for the door to their daughter's delight. "We'll buy a bigger sailboat."

"Daddy, you're supposed to carry Mommy *in* not *out!*"

"Rules are made to be broken, Jenny. Especially on your wedding day!"

He thought of the years without Megan, without Jenny, without the baby on its way, then tried to imagine a future without them at the center of it all. He couldn't. They filled his life the same way they filled his heart and he knew that the best years of his life were yet to be.

"Poor Jake." Megan nuzzled against the side of his neck. "Your life will never be the same."

"I know," he said, as they stepped out into the sunshine. "Remind me to thank you tonight."

Life was good.

And Jake Lockwood was a happy man.

Escape to a place where a kiss is still a kiss...
Feel the breathless connection...
Fall in love as though it were
the very first time...
Experience the power of love!

Come to where favorite authors—such as
*Diana Palmer, Stella Bagwell,*
*Marie Ferrarella* and many more—
deliver heart-warming romance and genuine
emotion, time after time after time....

*Silhouette Romance—*
stories straight from the heart!

*Where love comes alive*™